THE DANCING LIGHTS

MIKE WILLIAMSON

Copyright © 2013 Mike Williamson

All rights reserved.

ISBN: 1483921220
ISBN-13: 9781483921228

Thank you too all of the people who made possible the impossible.

CHAPTER ONE

James Nettles was a tramp! He was also an alcoholic. There was a time when he held down a reasonable job, had a wife and kids but it wasn't a happy marriage and when they left, his drinking increased and he became lost in a dream world of alcohol and drugs; a warm, comfortable world that had no worries or cares. So he lost his job and his home!

He joined the multitude of similarly unfortunate people who lived, or rather existed beneath the conscious level of normal society. The whiskey and vodka was replaced with bottles containing liquids of an uncertain nature and the drugs became powders of an unknown source.

The byways between Chester and Bristol were his haunts; he crossed between Wales and England, a shambling, mumbling, scarecrow caricature of a human being, unaware of the weather, time, or place. When opportunity arose, he would steal food and clothes, and usually slept under a damp hedge when he couldn't find a shed or barn.

Sometimes he was rescued from a shop doorway. Comatose and helpless, he was taken to a hospital but this just prolonged his misery. After recovering, he was usually released to continue his wretched life. From time to time he would be taken to an institute to purge his body of the toxic poisons, but always he was released back into the senseless void.

He arrived on his latest journey not too far from the historic town of Shrewsbury on a dark and filthy night, the sort of night that is common on the Welsh borders at the turn of the seasons. Ignoring the possibility of discovery and abuse, or the painful fangs of guard dogs, he sought shelter in a barn full of hay bales, to him a simple luxury. Making a nest in the bales, he pulled from his pocket a turnip, requisitioned from a nearby field, and proceeded to eat it. Not a simple thing as his teeth, the very few blackened and twisted that remained in his head, could hardly cope with the tough flesh of the vegetable.

As he ate, smacking his lips noisily, he gazed around his temporary home. In the dim light from the distant farmhouse, he could just make out a pair of pigeons, nestled high up in the roof. They eyed their new companion and shuffled nervously. They seemed to know that when in days gone by he had been able to catch one, it was a raw and tasty feast!

His eyes shifted and a smile pulled his face to one side. His friends were here! A ball of swirling lights hovered nearby, dancing and weaving patterns of light in the darkness of the night.

He couldn't remember when he first saw them, probably on a night like this one while he rested in another barn, or under a bridge. They did him no harm and provided the only companionship he ever had or wanted, a joyous, warmth of colour and movement.

In his feeble mind he could hear them singing, like angels come to entertain their friend. With his free hand, he waved as though conducting an orchestra and from his broken mouth he uttered notes of formless music.

Tired of trying to eat the impossible turnip, he threw it aside and used both hands, his dry eyes shining in the joy he felt, his whole body swaying to the rhythm only he could hear. From deep inside his ragged overcoat he drew forth a stained bottle and ignoring the noxious smell, he emptied it into his mouth. With half of the bottle consumed, it fell from his grasp and emptied out into the straw with a gurgle. His hands stopped waving, his eyelids drooped and his head slumped forward.
What dreams he may have had; we can only hope that he was whisked away in some long forgotten memory of happier, sunnier days. The mumbled song decayed into drunken snores as he ran in open fields, young and healthy once more. For a while, the ball of lights played on, before fading into the long, still night. The farm hand found him in the morning. At first he thought that the tramp was dead, but then he snored. They

summoned an ambulance and the crew recognised their 'Jimmy' from an earlier time. Carefully, they loaded him into the ambulance.

In the hospital, the doctor accurately diagnosed the cause of the unconsciousness. With a sigh, the doctor prescribed a bed and a drip until the patient came round. Then they would clean and feed him, but they could never clean the torment from his mind. Or the music of the dancing lights.

CHAPTER TWO

The young woman had bought a ready-cooked chicken breast from the store around the corner on her way home from work and thought that it would go well with a tossed salad, and it was while she was slicing the tomatoes that she became aware of something disturbing.

At first it was just a tiny speck of green light hovering in the corner of her eye and when she turned her head, it had disappeared. "Bother, I'll have to stop straining my eyes by reading in bed!" she muttered to herself, and then modified her resolution, "or at least not for half the night!" She dismissed it and attacked the tomatoes again.

A few days later the speck had returned, this time with a few friends of all colours. She was doubly annoyed as she had resisted reading her latest novel at all and allowed her eyes to rest but the pesky thing had returned, and then some!

Mary Kingman then became worried that it might be something more serious than eye strain. For a couple of weeks she tried to ignore the intermittent lights, but her friends began to ask if she was alright, and then she realised she was developing a nervous twitch in anticipation of the lights reappearance.

She had reasoned that as a nearly thirty year old woman, Mary was hardly at the age where serious things normally happened, and as she had a sedentary occupation, she regularly went to the gym and controlled her diet. She had the example of the other secretaries in the office that had developed a Grecian stoop and a wide posterior from not looking after themselves. Mary had a good figure and meant to keep it that way!

She also realised that she was not entirely happy at work. Her boss, Mr Priestly, was a sweet old guy and the others didn't cause any problems for her, but she felt that she was going nowhere. Perhaps she should think about extending her education and then she could find a different job. The problem was in choosing the right subject.

She decided that she needed a check-up before doing anything more, so she asked Priestly if she could have a morning off to see her doctor.

"My dear girl, of course you can," the old man said, his face puckered with concern, "I hope that it's not something too serious!"

"No, I feel just a bit rundown," Mary smiled confidently and brushed her mousy hair from her shoulders, "I'd rather sort this out than let it linger on. It could be just a touch of 'flu or something."

Priestly looked relieved and ran his hand over his bald pate, "Of course my dear, you run off and see the doctor and don't worry about a thing."

The doctor drew a blank. "I can't find anything wrong," he said, "We can send you for a scan to see if there is anything there, and I'll take a few blood samples. I'll do that now and you should receive an appointment for the scan in a few weeks."

Old Priestly looked worried when he heard the word 'scan'; to his age-group that had the ominous sound of something to be avoided, "I do hope that it's nothing serious," he repeated and looked out of the window at the falling rain, "Of course it's a bad time of year; shorter days and bad weather is depressing. You have some holidays due; perhaps you should take a short holiday in the sun somewhere."

Mary gave him a cheerful smile, almost sorry to have caused the old man to worry, "No thanks, it's probably nothing. I'll wait until after the scan."

On the way home she stopped off at the supermarket and bought the makings for a salmon dinner and a bottle of wine. Perhaps a good meal and relaxing with a glass of vino would do the trick, perhaps more than a glass. And she decided that she would continue reading her novel.

CHAPTER THREE

Mary was on her second glass of wine. She was relaxed after the meal; the dinner things were washed and replaced in the cupboard and drawers. She had turned off all the lights, except the hall and her reading lamp by the sofa, and dressed herself in a comfortable tracksuit.

For some time she hadn't noticed the annoying lights and thought that the answer must be in the wine and good food that had relaxed her; that it was probably an indication that she was more stressed than she had thought. She picked up the story line from where she had left off previously and snuggled into the sofa and its cushions, her feet tucked underneath her. The book was an Elizabethan drama and she became absorbed in the story of treachery and treason.

The appearance of a finger broke her concentration! It appeared slowly at first, just as a shadow of dots and then it assembled itself and crept across the page as though following the line of print. At least it looked like a finger but it was incomplete and not attached to a hand. It was comprised of hundreds, or perhaps thousands of the multi-coloured lights but with gaps, so that she could see through it and she was sure that she could see the sinews, veins and muscle and even the bone!

She gasped and dropped the book and the finger disappeared with a faint pop. She had been brought up as a Christian without any undue emphasis on the subject, so she wasn't religious and early in her childhood it soon became obvious to her that the biblical miracles were impossibilities and that included ghosts, spirits, and phantoms, but she was certain that she had seen something like a finger! She felt her previous convictions start to crumble away.

She looked hard at the glass of wine and wondered if she was intoxicated but emptied the glass in one swallow anyway! She could feel goose bumps and the hair on her neck standing up and her hands shook a little. She clenched her fists to control them and stood up and turned on every light in her apartment. She even checked the closet and under the bed to see if anyone or anything was there. And then she laughed! What would she have done if she had found a finger beckoning to her?

Then she let out a scream as something thumped heavily at the window! With faltering steps she approached the window and nervously peeked through the curtain. On the windowsill sat a pigeon, staring up at her with one bright red eye. She had been holding her breath and now let it out in a rush. The trouble with living in a brightly-lit city was that the birds kept flying through the night.

"It's about time you went to sleep!" she told the bird and that also seemed to be good advice for herself. She felt so nervous that she kept the tracksuit on and crawled into bed. She thought about her problem and decided that she should at least get out of the apartment and take the advice of Priestly to go somewhere for the weekend, somewhere in the country. Then she noticed that she had left all of the lights on. She shrugged and turned on her side and closed her eyes.

Then her eyes flew open! She realised that if there was something medically wrong with her, she would have seen the lights even with her eyes closed and that had never happened! With a brief satisfactory smile, she settled down and closed her eyes again but it was some time before she fell asleep.

CHAPTER FOUR

Christchurch is a pleasant place, even in the depths of winter, and typical of the English weather, it never stopped raining on the journey down. Mary had endured the torture of the hospital scan, (why were they so noisy?) and now waited for the results. After work on the Friday, Mary had taken her BMW Mini out of the garage she rented and checked it over. She rarely used it as most of what she did, travelling to work and shopping, could be done on foot or a short bus-ride. She filled the tank and blew some air into the tyres at the nearest filling station and set off for the south coast.

Her parents, now deceased, had taken her on holiday in that area many times in her youth and she had fond memories of the coast and the New Forest. It had been some years since she had been there, not since she was at school and she was impressed, and also a little disappointed in the motorways that had appeared since then; impressed that she found herself at her destination so quickly and disappointed that a lot of the charm of the old roads was now just a part of history. It did not stop her remembering the journey on the old roads, with her father breaking into song and encouraging everyone to join in. He sang in mock Italian and that caused a great deal of laughter on their journey!

She found a reasonable Bed & Breakfast; she had a lot of choice as it was out of season, run by a middle aged couple who were only too happy to rent her a room. She had a light supper with the couple and went to her room. At no time since leaving home had she been troubled with the specks of light or the frightening finger, so she went to bed without anticipating any trouble. She calculated that if she starting in the morning, she would have two full days to explore her childhood memories.

She was surprised at breakfast to find that she was not the only guest; a young man sat at the breakfast table while drinking coffee and staring moodily at the inclement weather through the bay window.

She hesitated and then walked up to the table, "Hi, we seem to be the only people staying here; do you mind sharing the table? I'm Mary."

The young man turned, startled and flustered by her voice but motioned for her to sit, "Please do, my name is Patrick," and then turned back to stare out of the window at the scudding clouds.

"I hope that I'm not intruding," Mary said as she sat down. She wondered about him, as his voice was fairly well cultured but he hadn't shaved that morning, or perhaps longer, and his hair was untidy and his dress was very casual.

He turned and stared blankly at her as the words registered and then shook his head, "No, not at all, I was just thinking. I'm sorry, it was rude of me; can I get you a cup of coffee, it's only instant I'm afraid."

"That would be very nice, thank you," She wondered how she could maintain the conversation but the decision was made for her.

Mrs Greenwood, their host, burst in from the kitchen carrying a tray, "Oh you're up and awake dear; I thought I heard you on the stairs. Would you be wanting a breakfast?" She laid the tray in front of Patrick.

Mary looked at what Patrick had ordered. It looked very unhealthy to her, but the smell of bacon and eggs made her mouth water, "Yes please, and I'll have the same as that!"

"Very good, I'll bring a full coffee pot for you both." Mrs Greenwood bustled away, only to return promptly with the coffee and a tray for Mary. "I suspected that you would need a good breakfast and had it ready. I think that it's the air that always makes our guests hungry."

Patrick shrugged, "There goes my chance of making a noble gesture!" He did manage to fill her coffee cup.

"How long have you been staying here?" Mary asked.

"Huh, about a week; needed some time to myself," he replied.

"Then I am intruding!" Mary said, appalled at her presumptive rudeness.

"Oh no, you're not!" Patrick assured her, "I just needed to be away from home for a while. I can assure you that you will not disturb me!" He crossed his heart, "Promise!"

"I felt the same," Mary nodded understandingly, "a change of air and scenery to recharge the batteries."

"That's it exactly!" Patrick smiled for the first time; "Shall we start again? Patrick Carmichael."

"Mary Kingman, nice to meet you Patrick," she stuck her hand out, and after a short hesitation Patrick shook it warmly.

"What are you going to do down here?" he asked.

"I used to come down here on holiday with my folks," Mary attacked her breakfast, "I thought that I'd visit some of those places, the ones I liked. What are you going to do?"

Patrick shrugged, "I just came to think, so I wasn't planning any trips."

"What have you done since you've been here?" She was surprised that anyone would come here and not explore.

"Stayed in my room most of the time, I've been to the pub a couple of times and looked around the town," Patrick looked a bit embarrassed at appearing so lazy.

"Well I'm going to look at the old fishing villages today," Mary looked out of the window, "and it looks as though the weather is improving. Would you like to come along?"

Patrick looked up from his breakfast. It was obvious that he had other things on his mind and was wrestling to make a decision, "Hell, why not? Perhaps a walk would do me some good. You're sure you don't mind?"

"Glad for the company!" Mary smiled, "Why did you choose to come here?"

Patrick gave a little chuckle, "I stuck a pin in a map!"

"And you've never been here before?" Mary was surprised.

"No, I've been to many places around the world but never here," he explained.

"You've missed some of the best scenery in England and some great history!" Mary observed, "There are some beautiful villages down here and the New Forest I find calming. At this time of year, everywhere will be peaceful and you'll think that you're in the seventeenth century."

"It's a deal then!" Patrick wiped his mouth on a napkin and picked up a camera from the window seat. Mary hadn't noticed it before. It looked very professional and Patrick noticed her surprise. "It's what I do, walk around taking snaps. I've just finished a contract and was wondering what to do next," he explained.

"It looks complicated!" Mary drained her coffee.

"I don't even think of it! I've been taking photographs since I was a lad in Manchester." He swung the camera around and clicked the shutter.

"Don't you need a flash when indoors?"

"A flash can rob the photograph of too much detail," He pointed at the window, "With this subdued lighting I can capture a mood."

CHAPTER FIVE

Mary didn't know why she had the impulse to invite a stranger to come along but he appeared pleasant enough, in a scruffy sort of way and she was intrigued as to what his problem was and why he had to come to a strange place to think things out. What things?

Patrick had similar thoughts. He had no intention of becoming friendly towards anyone while he was here, not even engaging in idle chatter and his acceptance of this woman's offer surprised him. Yes, he could see that she was very attractive and obviously well-educated and pleasant but his decision was still surprising. He decided that her auburn hair must be the reason; he appreciated the shade and the way it changed in the sunlight and he decided to get in a few shots of that beautiful hair before the day was over.

Perhaps it was their situation. As the only two people in the boarding house it meant that they couldn't avoid each other, not without appearing churlish. Also perhaps it was because he had been wrestling with the questions on his mind all week and getting nowhere and her company may just distract him enough to find the answers.

He was further surprised moments later, when she walked past her car and continued up the road.

"I want to see the river," she explained, "We used to spend a lot of time here and there used to be a good view from the bridge of the river and what people were doing."

He caught up to fall into step beside her and she continued talking, "In the fishing season there would often be a row-boat tied to both banks and a couple of men fishing for sea-trout. There was a lot of fish and I once saw a large trout jump out of the water and into the boat."

Patrick laughed, "Who was the more surprised, the fish or the fishermen?"

Mary laughed with him, "I think it must have been the fish!"

They arrived at the bridge and gazed down into the River Avon. Mary looked disappointed, "Well, I know that it is out of season but it's not as busy as I would have expected!"

Two boats were moving slowly in the distance and there was a little activity on the boats moored along the jetties; they could see a few heads bobbing up occasionally.

"I don't know a lot about sailing but I think that during the winter the owners repair and update the boats, prepare them for the summer," Patrick suggested as he brought the camera up to his eye and took a shot of the two boats, including Mary's hair blowing in the slight breeze.

Mary nodded, "You're probably correct but it was so much different in the summer then; people would be walking everywhere; women and girls in bright frocks and shorts, eating ice cream and having a good time but this is almost depressing!"

"Perhaps if we drive somewhere it will be better," Patrick suggested.

Slowly they retraced their steps and got into Mary's mini. "Have you got a car?" she asked.

Patrick pulled a face, "It's an old Ford and it broke down coming here. It's in a garage on the edge of town."

Mary laughed, "At least it got you to where you were going!"

"Not really, I was just driving round without a destination."

"So you had to stop here! Karma! It could have been worse!" Mary started the engine and pulled away, "I was thinking of looking at Keyhaven."

"Where's that?" Patrick asked.

"A small village on the other side of Lymington; it's cute and cosy and you can walk along the sea-wall." She looked sideways at her companion to check if that was a suitable choice.

"If there's a pub there, I'll buy you lunch!" Patrick confirmed with a promise, "All of this walking is going to make me ravenous!"

They pulled into the car park overlooking Keyhaven Harbour.

"Well, this is a bit different to what I remember!" Mary said as they left the car, "it's a larger car park and surfaced, other than that there isn't a lot of difference in the village."

"And the sun's out, so you should feel less disappointed," Patrick said, shading his eyes with his hand.

"It's actually a lot prettier in the dawn and sunset; the light on the water makes everything softer," Mary stood looking thoughtfully, briefly lost in some distant memory. "The pub's there," she pointed, "and we can start along the seawall from the end of the car park. Keyhaven was originally Anglo-Saxon and I believe it means 'where the cows sailed from'."

"You're not at tour-guide in your spare time are you?" Patrick teased her.

"I'm just curious and my dear father appeared to know everything! He used to teach history and took great delight in telling me strange little stories." Mary took his arm and pulled him towards the pathway. "That was one of them."

"What do you do for a living?" Patrick asked.

"I'm an accountant in a law firm; very boring!" She paused and leaned on the sea wall, looking back at the village, "What are you going to do next?"

"Not a great deal at the moment!" Patrick joined her to lean over the wall, "I've just finished a tour working with the army. I've been following the troops around. It's a bit grim at times and I became sick at some of the sights, so I want to photograph something else but I don't have any idea what at the moment."

"That was the last thing on my mind when we met! So you're a kind of war correspondent?" Mary took another look at his sandy hair and straight nose with a new respect. "I can understand that it has become something to avoid and why you're taking time off to think. Was it that experience that prompted you to just start wandering?"

"Probably, you reach a saturation point and can't take any more. It wasn't all bad though," Patrick took a deep breath, as though to expel the memories, "I got to go to places that few others get the chance to see and there were some really remarkable scenes and people. Now I want to photograph something that is natural!"

"Like those photographs in the National Geographic; I think that they are stunning!" Mary held both hands as though handling a picture frame, "How do they get all of that detail? I'm afraid that my attempts are too often out of focus and look confused! I have hundreds of headless snaps!"

Patrick nodded, "That's the sort of thing! I thought that if I wandered around, I might get some inspiration. As to your attempts, it takes a great deal of practice to take a good snap. Next time, take a deep breath and a second look before shooting."

"What are your initial thoughts so far?" Mary changed subject.

"That I should buy a new car!" Patrick changed the mood.

"About the photography, silly!" Mary poked her elbow in to his ribs.

Patrick dropped a pebble into the water and watched the ripples disappear under the bridge. "I'd really like to get on to a really fantastic project that would change people's lives."

"That sounds a grand idea!" Mary said enthusiastically.

"There are not so many grand projects around at the moment, at least not one that I could just walk into. An alternative is to extend my education; at least it would fill in the time until something did turn up."

"I would think that if you were already in a company, you would be in place when the opportunity arose," Mary pointed out another alternative.

"That's why I was thinking of going back to university! You hear of all sorts of opportunities on the grapevine." Patrick stood up straight and stretched, "Now I think we should go to the pub and get that lunch; it must be the sea air that's making me hungry!"

"Afterwards we can go and look at Hurst Castle; it's over there near that lighthouse." Mary pointed at a misty image in the distance.

CHAPTER SIX

They ordered fish dinners and a bottle of white wine at the inn and Patrick continued talking while they ate.

"So what's your problem?" Patrick looked up and stared directly into her eyes, "You've heard my story, and so what's yours?"

Mary poised with her glass halfway to her mouth; the question had surprised her. From the moment that she had left her apartment, there had been no strange specks of light or moving ghostly fingers and she had almost forgotten about them! She set the glass down and studied it for a moment. How could she explain her experience to a man who dealt with real things, like war and death?

"I was just wondering at breakfast if you were a nut but if I tell you my problem you'll almost certainly think I'm certifiable!" She looked up to watch his reaction.

"I can be the judge of that!" Patrick answered, "But first tell me a bit more about yourself; do you live alone?"

"Is that a way of asking if I have a boyfriend? No, I haven't at present; the last one was over two years ago," Mary took a sip from her glass, "When I started working I had a flatmate, another girl for financial reasons, but when I got a better salary I moved to where I am now. I don't have parents or any siblings but there is a cousin in Canada that I haven't seen for years. The job I have is secure and well paid and I have a kind old boss and the work is enough to keep me busy without any undue stress."

"That does not appear to mirror the life of most single young women, and you're lucky not to be stressed out as many girls are, with their jobs or boyfriends," Patrick observed, "So what could be troubling you?"

Mary folded her hands on the table and looked at them, "You're probably going to think that I should be in a lunatic asylum! A couple of months ago I began to see coloured lights out of the corners of my eye. I thought that I had been reading too much and put it down to eye-strain but I went to see my doctor who told me that my eyes looked okay. The coloured lights continued and even increased in number - and then I saw what looked like a weird finger!"

"Just a finger? Describe it to me!" Patrick became very attentive and didn't show any signs of disbelief.

"It was incomplete and I could see the bones and tissues and it was made up of the same coloured lights." Mary looked up to read her companion's expression and was surprised and relieved to see that he appeared to be taking her seriously.

"What was the finger doing?" he asked.

"I was reading at the time and the finger appeared to be following the text, as though it was also reading!" Mary's face became tense as she recalled the event, even a tick appeared in her cheek.

"What happened next?" Patrick's voice had a calming effect.

Mary pulled a face, "I blew it! I dropped the book and probably screamed and the finger disappeared! I was so nervous that I kept the lights on all night but as I tried to sleep I suddenly realised that I never saw the lights while my eyes were closed."

Patrick pulled on his lower lip, "I assume that you're not usually a nervous person and you don't have a brain tumour. I think that when your eyes are closed and the lights don't appear is significant; if you had a medical problem, they would probably be more noticeable when your eyes were closed."

"That's what I thought but there's more; since I left my apartment to come here, I haven't seen anything at all!" Mary said positively and sat back with her hands in her lap.

Patrick also sat back and gave the problem some thought before replying, "Have the lights appeared anywhere else, or has anyone else seen them?"

Mary shook her head, "I've never seen them outside of my apartment!"

"How do you travel to work?"

"Mostly by bus or walking; I never use the car, as almost everything is fairly close to the apartment. You don't think I'm going mad then?" She looked calmer for telling the story to a perfect stranger and who even more importantly, appeared to accept it.

Patrick shook his head, "It sounds like one of those strange ghost stories! You don't happen to be very religious do you?"

It was Mary's turn to shake her head, her auburn hair flying in all directions, "I think that religion is just superstition and I don't believe in ghosts!"

Her companion mused over the story, "It only appears when you are doing your normal activities but broke off when you did something unusual and got in the car to come here. You've only seen the finger once?" Mary nodded.

"Barring medical reasons, specks of light are photons and that is in my field of interest. Could you describe the finger as anything else other than a finger?" Patrick asked.

Mary shook her head, "I could even see what looked like a finger nail!"

"Would you mind if I accompany you back to your flat?" Patrick held up a cautionary finger, "purely in the name of research."

Mary hesitated; she was used to her solitary existence and the thought of sharing with a perfectly strange man, even for a few days, made her feel uncomfortable. On the other hand she felt nervous at returning to the empty apartment.

Patrick realised that she had a doubt, "It seems only fair that I help you with your problem, even if it is only a ghost!"

Mary made up her mind, "I wouldn't dismiss it as 'only a ghost'. If you don't mind sleeping on the sofa, you're welcome."

Patrick smiled, "I also promise to put the toilet seat down! We can pick up my car on the way but we may as well finish your holiday first. Where is this castle you mentioned?"

CHAPTER SEVEN

Patrick's car was ready, so after he had picked it up at the garage, they travelled in convoy back to her apartment. They had to park his old Ford in the street and it would have to be moved every day but Mary thought that there was a garage next to hers that was free for hire – if Patrick stayed for more than a few days.

The first thing that Patrick did was to inspect the apartment. "I was wondering if there could be another reason for the lights but it looks okay to me. How are the neighbours?"

"Quiet and respectable," Mary answered, "Most of them are retired and I only hear anything when their grandchildren come to visit."

"Huh, huh, you read a lot!" Patrick examined the titles of some of the books in the bookcase.

"I guess that it's biological," Mary fluffed up one of the sofa's cushions, "My parents had a whole room devoted to books and they even spilled over into the rest of the house. I grew up with books."

Patrick took his outer jacket off and looked round for somewhere to put it.

"There is an inbuilt wardrobe in the hall," said Mary noticing his unspoken question. "Do you want a meal? I can cook something simple or we can go to a restaurant."

Patrick found the wardrobe and hung his coat, "I'm not that hungry but if you don't want to cook we could eat out or get a takeaway."

"I'll make some sandwiches." She decided, "Do you want tea or coffee?"

"Whatever you're having and sandwiches sound perfect!" Patrick re-entered the living room and resumed looking for sources for peculiar lights.

"Sit down and you can turn on the TV or radio; I haven't a clue as to what's been happening!" Mary turned towards the kitchen.

Patrick turned on the TV and examined it in case it was emitting stray visible photons from somewhere else other than the screen. Mary entered with two plates of sandwiches.

"I wasn't sure of what you liked, but I have tuna in one and beef paste in the other. Coffee should be along in a moment." She looked at Patrick who had his head round the back of the TV, "I usually see the programmes better from the front!"

Patrick looked sheepish as he turned round, "I was just wondering if the source of the lights could be the TV."

"I hardly have it on and it wasn't when I saw the finger." She disappeared into the kitchen again and returned with a coffee-pot and cups.

They sat opposite each other at the coffee table. Patrick helped himself to a sandwich from each plate.

"We have to sort out a campaign so that we can both see what is happening. When and if anything appears again, don't be scared and frighten it off; call me quietly. No sudden movements!" He then took a bite at a sandwich.

"That's easier said than done!" Mary said as she poured the coffee, "You should have a finger appear out of nowhere!"

"That's what I'm hoping will happen!" Patrick mumbled around his mouthful.

CHAPTER EIGHT

Their anticipation waned as the days passed and Mary had nothing to report, not even a single speck of light. She went to work as usual and Patrick bought and set up a security camera. It was on the tenth day that something happened: Mary arrived home to find her guest in a state of excitement.

Patrick was pointing at the laptop with a shaking finger, "There, I caught it on camera!"

Mary looked at the screen and frowned, "I can't see anything!"

"There in the corner of the room! You see that everything is in sharp focus, except that area about the size of a football."

"Are you sure that it's not a fault in the computer or a thumbprint on the lens? What I saw was coloured lights and that is grey and out of focus." Mary didn't look convinced but bent to look closer at the monitor.

"But I saw it, and it was coloured, and it moved; look as I run the sequence," Patrick pressed a key and the almost transparent fuzzy area moved across the room, "I think that the camera can't pick up the colours for some reason but it proves that you're not going bonkers!"

Mary was still not convinced and sat down next to Patrick. "I never thought that I was going bonkers but it still does not look like the things I saw!"

"I'll have to get some more gear to pick up different wavelengths," Patrick wasn't put out by her lack of enthusiasm, "I think that they are only just in the range of visible light and that's why it just looks fuzzy and grey!"

"And you saw coloured lights?" Mary asked and Patrick nodded with a big grin on his face. She looked round the room, "I can't see anything now!"

"When you first told me of the lights, I had a few doubts but now you doubt me! They were there and when I get the new gear, we'll both be satisfied!"

"Hmm, do you want to eat out tonight?" Mary returned to practical matters.

For the first time Patrick looked deflated, "I think that we've made progress but you're not at all convinced! I thought that you would be excited!"

"I haven't seen anything for two weeks and I'm beginning to think that I just needed a break and it has worked!" Mary admitted, "When you can record what I saw, then I'll be convinced! Now, shall we eat out?"

The next evening she returned to find Patrick surrounded by electronic boxes and reading one of a pile of books he had dumped on the coffee table.

"I've bought a new camera," he announced and pointed to a larger camera next to the earlier one on the bookcase, "with this gear it will pick up almost all wavelengths and I'm boning up on physics."

Mary picked up a book from the coffee table and read the title, "You're really hooked into this! I didn't expect you to go to this extent!"

"There's a lot that has been happening since I last studied the subject, so I'm bringing myself up-to-date." He waved an open book in her face.

"Anything else happened today?" Mary felt embarrassed that Patrick had become absorbed in her problem and had bought what was obviously an expensive piece of equipment on her behalf.

Patrick shook his head, "All very quiet as far as our little friends are concerned. I'm curious as to why they do not hang around all the time; you would think that once they had arrived, they would stay."

"They were constantly with me all the time," Mary pulled a face, "Perhaps because I was absent it broke the connection."

"I had thoughts in that direction," Patrick laid the book down, "They never followed you to the office and the doctor's surgery, but as soon as you changed the pattern by not being here every day, they disappeared."

"I'm not sure if I want them to re-appear!" Mary grimaced.

The following morning they did! Patrick was in the kitchen preparing the morning coffee when he heard Mary call out. He walked into the living room and followed her voice to the bathroom.

"It's in here!" she called out as calmly as possible, "Come in, I'm almost decent!"

Patrick slowly opened the door and saw Mary standing in the shower with a towel carelessly clutched to her front. He had time to confirm that she was very attractive before following her outstretched hand to a group of dancing lights. He slid into the room.

"Blast! For obvious reasons I didn't put a camera in here!" he exclaimed.

The multi-coloured lights were shifting and at first it reminded him of dust motes dancing in sunlight but then he noticed that the movements were more organised than dust in a draught. They formed almost rigid patterns and as he watched the group split in two and performed a pas de deux.

"I've got an idea," Mary stepped out of the shower, "Wait outside while I get dressed."

Patrick took one last admiring look at her and slid out into the passage. Mary came out after a few minutes wearing a dressing gown and the towel now wrapped like a turban on her head. She didn't rush but slowly walked back in to the living room with Patrick following. Mary sat on the sofa, while

Patrick stood in the middle of the room with a puzzled expression on his face.

"Look!" Mary nodded to the door behind Patrick and he turned to see that the coloured lights had followed her into the room.

"Well, I'll be damned!" Patrick's mouth fell open.

"I remembered what we were talking about yesterday; that they appeared to follow me and this shows that they do!" Mary continued to dry her hair with the towel, "As long as they find me they can follow but when I went to the car they must have lost contact."

Slowly Patrick sat next to Mary while keeping a watch on the lights. "I feel a bit nervous about that!" he said quietly, "It shows a level of intelligence. They have worked out your routine and can find you anywhere within that routine. They were not aware of your car and that's why they lost contact!"

Mary stopped rubbing her hair and looked at her guest with one eye through a gap in her hair. "That's about as stupid as ghosts and angels! I was thinking more on the lines of magnetism."

Patrick shook his head, "No, it couldn't be magnetism because your magnetism wouldn't be that different to mine or anyone else's but it keeps coming back to you. It's an intelligent selection!"

Mary's hair had cascaded over her face and she blew a hole through it to see him better, "I would prefer a ghost!"

"The camera is recording but we can see if the new gear has made any improvements," Patrick eased the laptop round and they looked at the screen.

"Oh!" Mary said softly, while Patrick never uttered a sound. He looked at the image on the screen and then at the lights moving in the room. Then he tapped a few keys and the screen image changed.

Eventually he spoke, also softly, "It's composed of more than we can see with our eyes. I changed the wavelength and it showed a different shape. Look, I'll change the wavelength again."

"What is it?" Mary clutched his arm.

Patrick shook his head, "I have no idea. Is that a head and is that an arm? If you saw a finger there should be a hand and an arm."

"Perhaps it isn't complete; I can still see through the outer surface." Mary pulled a face.

"Is there an outer surface?" Patrick said softly. "It is shifting around so much that I cannot make out if there is an outer boundary."

"It keeps changing shape!" Mary complained, "I can't make out what it should be. That thing you said could be an arm has split into two, or is it three?"

"I would guess that its shape is something we are not familiar with," Patrick muttered.

Mary looked at him, "Do you have an idea of what it is?"

"I have several ideas but I suspect that none of those guesses comes anywhere near the truth!" Patrick kept tapping the keys and searching through the spectrum for another shape.

"Are we going to sit here all night watching it?" Mary gave up drying her hair.

"Hmm, it could go on for days. Can you get up and go into the kitchen; make some more coffee or something," Patrick suggested.

With one last look at the screen, Mary rose and edged nervously into the kitchen, all the while keeping an eye on the lights.

"It's drifting towards you but don't worry, it hasn't hurt you yet," Patrick informed her.

"It's the 'yet' part that worries me!"

"It's hovering just outside of the kitchen door and making no effort to go through. I'm standing now and walking over to the window," Patrick kept up a running commentary, "Now it's changed shape again and coming slightly towards me. Now it's just hovering there, as though it's watching both of us."

"Huh, don't say that!" Mary's voice rose a degree or two, "The thought that it can see us makes my skin crawl!" She returned with two mugs of coffee.

Patrick moved back and sat at the laptop and punched some more keys. Mary sat next to him.

"What are you doing now?" she asked.

"I'm zooming in to get a close-up." He kept moving the camera. "They move around a lot more than you think, and do you notice, they're transparent and close up the colour is very faint."

"What do you make of them?" Mary set the mugs down.

Patrick placed his chin in both hands, "I haven't a clue! They're not solid but appear to be attached to each other somehow and they are aware of us; they followed you into the kitchen and came back when I moved to the window."

Mary shuddered, "Are you telling me that they are intelligent?"

"Not necessarily. I know that I said that earlier but there could be a number of reasons that they are attracted to us," he said thoughtfully.

"You mean like magnetism?"

"There are a number of forces that act in the same way as magnetism," Patrick replied, "We need some more equipment but they cost a lot more than I can afford. I'll have to borrow them."

"Borrow them; from where?" Mary asked.

"I'll make some 'phone calls tomorrow and see what I can do. I have friends!" Patrick gave her a confident smile.

"Is that legal?" She asked. She had a feeling that Patrick would bend a few rules.

Patrick shrugged his shoulders, "As long as it's not needed urgently, they'll never know and I won't need them for long."

Mary looked again at the cloud of lights that had now returned to their original position. "You want more gadgets to find out more; what sort of things do you want to know?"

"I will have to talk to someone to answer that fully, but we need to know about atmospheric changes and any radiation that may be flying around," Patrick placed a hand on Mary's arm, "There is radiation all the time and it is mostly harmless but I would like to know what is really here; nothing to worry about!"

"I'm not worried, as at least if you can see it and the camera records it and that proves I'm not going nuts!" Mary said happily.

"I never said that you were nuts!" Patrick smiled gently at her. "If I had thought that, I would not have come here."

CHAPTER NINE

The following evening Patrick had an announcement, "I spoke to a friend I met in college, he was a lecturer then and now he's a full blown professor and this is just up his street. He has the equipment but I'll have to pick it up." He looked at Mary questioningly, "It means that I'll be gone all day tomorrow; will you be okay if the lights come back?"

"I'll be fine; now I know that it's not just me." Mary replied with a comforting smile.

"Good! I'll pick the stuff up tomorrow," Patrick looked relieved.

He drove up to Manchester the following morning and found his friend waiting and surrounded with boxes and cables. They loaded the Ford and the gear took up all of the space. He then had a lecture on how to use the equipment, a long lecture, plus he was given a number of books.

Mary returned home to find that Patrick had started to install the equipment.

"What is all this stuff?" Mary gestured to the boxes and coils of cables.

"At the moment it is nothing, but when I have assembled everything it will become a multiple sensor and will measure everything in this room." He picked up a cable and inserted the end into one of the boxes, "I hope that this does not inconvenience you."

"I just want answers!" Mary replied, "Can I make you some tea or coffee?"

When Mary returned with the refreshments, Patrick turned to her, "You will have to be careful where you walk, as unfortunately there will be many cables crossing the floor."

Mary sat in the armchair and kept clear of the activity, "What does this do?"

"What this does is to measure differences in different parts of the room; things like temperature, pressure and stray radiation. Normally there would be little difference; no changes during the day, or even several days, but we have to make sure. What do you want to do this evening?"

"Oh, we could watch TV, or read, or go out for a meal," Mary thought that it sounded boring and she wanted to see the equipment work.

"Reading is fine, but the TV might interfere with this equipment; even the lighting will make a problem, but I can allow for them." Patrick looked at her to see if she understood, "Even our walking about will make changes as it's very sensitive equipment."

"So we have to sit still all night?" Mary was astonished.

"No, no, but if we rush around for every minute, it will make it difficult to interpret the results." Patrick held up some paperbacks, "I've bought a couple of novels just for this occasion."

"Does your friend have any idea of what causes it?" Mary asked.

Patrick shook his head, "He refuses to comment until he knows more and I didn't say anything about shapes and fingers! I think everything's hooked up now." He looked around to see if he had forgotten anything.

Mary inspected the festoon of cables, "I feel hooked up!"

"Just let me set the ambient conditions and then we can have that meal."

CHAPTER TEN

It was almost a week later that the specks of lights came back and in a spectacular way! Mary had gone out briefly to the corner shop to buy some milk and Patrick was in the kitchen making the coffee when an alarm went off; something that he had hooked into the system to indicate there had been a change in the ambient conditions was telling him something.

He walked into the living room and couldn't see anything, so he checked the equipment. According to the gauges there was a surge but there was nothing to see. Mary returned to find Patrick standing tense and motionless in the centre of the room. He held up a finger indicating that silence was required.

After a few moments he slowly turned round, "The alarm went off but I can't see anything. We'll just continue as normal and see if anything appears."

Mary finished making the coffee and they settled down on the sofa, not really relaxed; their gaze travelling around the room. Her eye fell on the flashing warning light: Patrick had silenced the sound and she pointed at it.

"There's some energy in the room; although I've reset the detectors they are still showing something more than usual," Patrick replied in a soft voice.

They had drunk half of the coffee and Patrick let out a soft sigh, "We could wait all night without anything appearing!" He reached for one of the novels and started reading. Mary just sat there, her mind drifting in thought. The warning light went out and Patrick read the instruments and grunted.

He sat back down and picked up the book, "It looks as though our friends have left."

Mary stirred herself and was about to answer when something new happened: there was a high frequency buzz, as though a large insect had flown into the room. The warning light blazed and all of the gauges showed a positive reaction.

Patrick's head whirled round trying to find the source of the noise; it seemed to rise and fall in a pattern but the source of the buzzing remained uncertain. Mary put out her hand to hold on to Patrick's arm.

Then the lights appeared! Not in hundreds or thousands, but in millions! They streamed out of a corner of the room; a galaxy of multi-coloured shooting stars that filled the whole room in a violent starburst, swirling round their heads and apparently passing through their bodies!

Mary buried her head in Patrick's shoulder, while his mouth gaped at the spectacle. The pitch of the buzzing deepened and the lights reversed their movement and fled back to the corner of the room to gather and hover in a formless shape. Then in an instant, everything vanished and the room became quiet again.

For some minutes they sat quietly, shocked into silence by the appearance of the unknown phenomenon. Mary recovered first but her voice shook, "Well, that was certainly something different!"

"Yeah, now we have sound!" Patrick tried to be flippant, realising that Mary was probably more startled than he.

"What happened?" Mary still hung on to Patrick's arm, "What was that? It was like nothing that happened before!"

Patrick looked at the gauges. "It was a larger burst of energy than before. I have no idea what is going on! We'll look at the action again and see if it shows something."

The replay showed exactly what they had seen and even when slowed down there were no clues as to why the specks of light acted differently. The laptop had also captured the buzzing sound but it just sounded like an angry wasp.

"Do you know what it reminds me of?" Mary said, "It's like when you turn music on but the volume is on max and then it's adjusted."

"Are you suggesting that it's a musical? It's not like any music I've heard!" Patrick frowned at the instruments as though they would speak and supply answers.

"Maybe not, but I'm glad you were here when it happened, or I would have really thought that I was going mad!" Mary's voice was still shaking.

Patrick checked the meters, "Well, all of the meters are showing normal readings, so we can relax for a while."

Mary couldn't resist a shiver, "I'm even less certain that I want to see it again!"

"I agree that it's startling but it hasn't done any physical harm as yet and probably never could. I think that is the last we'll see of it tonight!" Patrick reached for his book and Mary picked up a magazine.

Patrick was wrong! He had used the bathroom in preparation for going to sleep and Mary had started to make her way to the bathroom when the buzzing started again. They both froze and looked towards the corner of the room.

The starburst appeared again but this time instead of filling the room, it confined itself to the corner, high up towards the ceiling. The specks of light flew out to the periphery of an ill-defined limit, swirled around forming a vortex and then returned to the source. There was an endless stream, or streams flowing back and forth, swirling and dancing to an unknown melody.

The buzzing deepened to become a growl, rising and falling as though from a strange animal. Some of the specks did not return to their source, instead they stopped at the boundary and lost their colour, becoming grey. Gradually a shape began to appear, a grey shifting shape that slowly evolved into a gigantic face reaching from floor to ceiling!

Mary crept close to Patrick and he automatically placed a protective arm around her shoulders. They stood and watched the apparition form and then lose cohesion, only to reform again. There were the usual gaps in the surface and it was unnerving to see the tongue, nasal passages and even parts of the brain. At one stage the eyes stood unsupported, floating in front of the face. Mary let out a small mew of surprised horror and Patrick's mouth opened in surprise. The face became clearer - and it resembled Mary!

CHAPTER ELEVEN

The face shimmered and then lost form as though it was struggling to maintain the appearance of Mary's face. It was shifting in and out of focus. The buzzing had become a deep, drawn-out moan, also changing in volume and intensity. It reminded Patrick of a singing dog.

Abruptly it stopped! The grey surface became individual coloured specks of light that sped back towards an invisible source, the face collapsing from the centre. The sound faded to end up as a small squeak.

As silence descended on the scene, Mary and Patrick still clung to each other, frozen into immobility by surprise and shock.

Patrick wiped his hand over his face and was surprised to find that he was sweating, "What the hell was that?" he muttered.

"What did it look like to you?" Mary whispered. Her eyes were wider and more frightened than they had been before.

"It looked a lot like you at times!" Patrick saw that she was really unsettled.

"That's what I thought! What is happening?" Mary's voice trembled and she found that her legs were too, so she sat down, almost collapsing and dragging Patrick down with her.

"I don't know but I think we'll have to recover our wits before we can rationalise that!" Patrick stroked her shoulder, trying to comfort her.

"I'm not going to sleep tonight! I'll make some chocolate and please don't leave me alone!" Mary begged.

They did sleep eventually, one at each end of the sofa; Mary twitching and mumbling in some nightmare of her own. The lights burned all night and in the morning they both looked haggard.

"I'll make some strong coffee," Patrick said as he stood and tried to relieve the stiffness in his joints, "Are you going into work today?"

Mary paused and then shook her head, "No! I'll ring in sick. I need to sort out this nightmare. Why me? Why did it use my face?"

"Go and wash up, even take a shower while I make the coffee; you'll feel better for it!"

She didn't shower but looked a lot fresher when she emerged from the bathroom. Patrick noticed the dark circles around her eyes and surmised that he could not have looked much better!

They drank the strong coffee in silence for a while, perhaps afraid to open up on the subject that was troubling them, or more than likely just confused as to where to begin.

"What do you make of it?" Mary eventually started the conversation.

"Although it was a shock, using your face need not be that alarming," Patrick said, "We had already surmised that it knew of our presence and this simply means that they can actually see us, or at least you. I think it was a message but from where or from whom, God alone knows!"

"What was the message?" Mary said shakily.

"Simply hello." Patrick surmised.

"I've news for them! I would have preferred a post card!" Mary gave an involuntary shudder.

"Someone is trying to contact you, or us," Patrick continued, "Maybe they used your face because it was something familiar to us and the only thing available to them."

"Why couldn't they use their own face?" There was a bite to her voice.

"What would you have felt if the face of a stranger entered your room?" Patrick reasoned.

"Hmm! I see your point but who is it and why?" Mary frowned, folding her arms protectively over her chest while glaring at the recording equipment on the coffee table, blaming them for the horror show.

"There is also how! It's quite a complicated way to send a message and we can assume that they can't send a letter or use a telephone, or they would have."

"That's weird! Anyone on the planet can send a message by the normal methods!" The bite was still in her voice.

"I think that you have answered yourself; anyone on the planet can but what if it does not originate on this planet!" Patrick looked firmly in her face.

Mary started laughing, her voice held a note of hysteria, "That's crazy! Little green men are trying to contact me!"

Patrick gave a small smile in response to her laughter, "Think of it: this is a very high tech method to send a message and if they were on this planet, they could use any of our systems with ease, so there must be a reason that they can't!"

Mary sobered up, "I can see your reasoning but I can't accept your supposition that it is from another world! In any case, why just me?"

"Perhaps this is the easiest place they can reach." Patrick was trying his best to formulate a rational explanation.

Mary shook her head, "None of this makes any sense; if they can reach me, surely they can reach others!"

"Maybe they have. Look at the method they are using," Patrick argued, "They are using photons to form an image and I think that the noise is a form of speech. Judging from the way that both of the image and sound shifted in and out of focus, it must be damn difficult to use."

"If we went to someone and said that little green men are trying to contact me by using lights, they would lock us up in a padded cell!" Mary gave a nervous giggle.

"I'll give you another thought," Patrick pointed to the corner of the room, "What if they are aliens? If they projected an image of themselves, it could be more frightening than the image of a strange human and for that reason they projected a friendly image, one that would not be a threat."

Mary relaxed, sitting back in the sofa and her arms unfolded, "You're almost convincing me but I can't accept that it is aliens! Perhaps it is some research project here on earth; that seems more reasonable to me!"

"If it were a research project, they would contact the receiver of the message before the experiment!" The logic of that was inescapable and Mary couldn't think of an answer but Patrick continued.

"Whatever this is, it is obviously created by an intelligence. This could not be caused by a random natural event if the sender is on this planet or even one of our people in space, they would have contacted you by a normal method by now and they haven't! I will concede that it could be a lone nutcase somewhere but that is unlikely, so that leaves just something trying to contact us from out there!" He waved his hand vaguely at the ceiling, "It tried not to alarm you too much by sending a familiar image! It wants to be friendly!"

"It hasn't succeeded!" Mary said with feeling, "I've never been so scared in my life!"

"But it is trying!" Patrick thumped his knee, "If it cannot contact you by normal means, this is the only way. We can add to that, that it is having problems in holding the signal and that leads to some of the scary things you've witnessed!"

Mary started picking at the hem of her blouse, "I can accept that some-THING is trying to make contact, but this is more like – a – a –séance than a radio message!"

"I think that it will become clearer as more messages are sent!" Patrick tried to sound more positive than he felt.

"I'm not ready to continue, whatever this is," Mary started crying, "I felt nervous when I suspected that I had a brain tumour and when I met you and you saw the same things, I felt better but the thought of aliens invading my privacy, my life!" She bent over and buried her face in her knees, her shoulders heaving with sobs.

Patrick felt uncomfortable; after all, it was his theory that had partly caused this outburst.

He tried to make amends, "Look, if you're up to it, we can go out somewhere, to just get out of here for a few hours!"

After a few more sobs, Mary lifted her tear-stained face, "I'll have that shower first and I'd like to see the gardens at Kew; it's a bit early but the gardens will be a distraction."

"That's great! I've never seen them!" He said brightly.

CHAPTER TWELVE

The walk in the gardens at Kew did relax Mary, although she acted nervously at any loud sound. As predicted, the flowers in the gardens had only just started to bud but there was a fine show of daffodils and the last of the snowdrops. The hothouses were as normal, full of tropical plants and this was where Mary really relaxed; perhaps it was because it represented another world, warm and moist as opposed to the outside chill and damp.

They took their time returning to the apartment; walking along the river until they found a café. They talked of all sorts of things, everything except what was really on their minds; inconsequential nonsense, stories from childhood, from school, of their friends, and their adventures.

Patrick's tales captivated Mary: they were of strange people in far away, exotic lands. He had a remarkable descriptive way of telling what he had seen and experienced. Mary remarked on this.

"I suppose that it's being a photographer," he explained, "There are two ways to photograph something; the first is to arrange it in a pleasing composition and the second is seeing something about to happen and catching it at just the right moment. That means that you have to see everything in small detail very quickly."

"I imagine that it takes time to develop that skill," Mary said.

"Time and patience! With animals it can sometimes be easier, as they often repeat the same action several times but humans are animals too and it is sometimes surprisingly easy to predict their next action." He looked at her, "How are you feeling now?"

"A lot better thanks!" Mary took his hand, "Thank you for being there for me."

Patrick laughed, "To tell the truth, I was just as shaken as you and needed to get out of there. Are you ready to see what happens next?"

"Yeah, let's see what appears. It might be your face!" Mary smiled finally at that thought.

They entered Mary apartment cautiously, listening for any noises. Patrick checked the gauges and saw that nothing had happened while they were away. They put away some provisions that they had bought on their way home and Mary put on some coffee. As they had eaten at the café, neither of them felt hungry but Mary brought in a plate of biscuits with the coffee.

"What shall we do now?" she asked.

"Just sit and wait! This must be very frustrating for you; don't you have friends to see, or things to do?" Patrick queried.

"I don't have many close friends and those that I do have are used to me wanting my own space. They will probably ring sometime to spread some gossip, girl talk. What about you?"

"Ah, just about the same. I'm often away for months at a time so they are used to my silence. I keep in touch with my good friends with an e-mail now and then." Patrick scratched his head in a thoughtful manner.

"What are you going to tell them about this?" Mary asked.

Patrick stopped! He hadn't thought about how he would describe this strange phenomenon. Meeting a strange but attractive girl while taking a short break and then helping her to solve this problem. "It won't be easy and there's not a lot to be said until we find out more."

"Do you mind if we watch TV? There's a programme that I would like to see." Mary reached for the newspaper to check the broadcast times.

"Not at all! I don't think it won't interfere with our strange guest. What's the programme about?" Patrick asked.

"History! It's about women in religion. Not too much for you, I hope!" Mary's face showed signs of breaking into laughter.

Patrick realised that her bright humour was a reaction against the unnerving events and that she was on the verge of some hysterical breakdown. "Strangely enough, that isn't such a bad idea. I spent some time in Italy and Vatican City years ago and there is more to ladies in the Church than just the Madonna."

So they watched the news and then the programme, or at least Mary watched it as Patrick was lost in thought and watched the instruments. The programme finished and Mary turned the TV off.

"That was interesting! I never knew that there was a Pope Joan! It must have created a lot of consternation in the Vatican!" She said.

Patrick roused himself from his thoughts. "I'm wondering what she looked like; I would imagine not very feminine, if no one realised."

"There are men with…." Mary was cut short by the sound of loud buzzing and they both looked expectantly towards the corner of the room where the apparition appeared last time.

Only the buzzing continued, rising and falling in a peculiar rhythm and then it faded. Then the specks of light appeared and this time in a torrent, millions of particles rushing towards them and filling every corner of the room and again apparently passing through their bodies! They both flinched and ducked, Mary letting out a cry of shocked surprise.

The torrent of light slowed and then fled back to the source and the buzzing restarted in its strange melody. As before, the specks of light lost their colour on the periphery of a grey-shifting surface. As before, it reached from floor to ceiling, forming the rough shape of a face but what a face! The eyes were vertically aligned, one above the other and the mouth was placed to one side of the eyes at a forty-five degree angle, while the nose appeared to be poking out of the top of the image! All of this was shifting, twisting, as though it was a tormented soul.

Mary's face had become chalky white, her eyes extended in horror. Patrick had screwed his face up against the blaze. Abruptly, the light returned to the source, the sound ceased and all became quiet once more.

"Wow! That was way out!" Patrick croaked. Mary said nothing, frozen to become an immobile statue.

As he bent to study the readings, he noticed that Mary's hands had started to shake. He quickly took her hands into his own and noticed that his were not too steady either.

"Hey, it's over! It hasn't hurt us, just given us a big surprise!"

The whole of Mary's body began to shudder, so he placed an arm around her shoulders, and pulled her in close. "There, there, take it easy; it's gone now."

Her breath came in short gasps and then it was replaced by sobbing. Patrick patted her and made small comforting noises.

Eventually she lifted her tear-stained face and looked into his, "That was terrifying! It was as though the room had exploded!"

"Well, it hasn't and all is exactly as it should be."

"Is it?" Mary buried her face in his shoulder. "That face was like something Picasso would have created from one of his nightmares!"

CHAPTER THIRTEEN

"How would you like to see a movie?" It was a couple of days after the second explosion of light and Mary was still acting nervously; Patrick thought that she needed a diversion.

"What's on?" She had a strong compulsion to get out of the apartment and found the section in the local newspaper that advertised cinema programmes.

"I would suggest something dramatic, but not a disaster movie!" Patrick suggested.

"You mean not Dracula's Bride!" Mary scanned down the list, "What about the theatre? I would love to see Mama Mia; all that lovely Abba music!"

"If we can get the tickets, that's fine. I saw the film and it was enjoyable." Patrick agreed.

"What were you doing watching a chic-flick?" Mary looked at him with a comically suspicious expression. "Is there something that you're not telling me?"

Patrick gave a short laugh, "I was with some friends and the guys were outvoted by the girls. I don't have any strange compulsions such as wearing your clothes!"

Mary rang up the ticket office and found that there were two tickets available and so arranged to pick them up at the theatre.

"What shall we wear?" Patrick picked at his jeans.

"I don't think that it matters. We can pretend that we're impoverished students. Come on, it'll be fun!" She seized his arm. Her forced gaiety a result of the tumult in her mind.

They took a bus from the same stop that Mary used to go to work; eventually it would bring them to the theatre. They took their seats and looked around. They must have hit the right time as there were empty seats and the only people standing were waiting to get off.

Their seats were sideways, under the windows and shared with a plump woman who gave a slight smile as they say down.

"Isn't it remarkable what they can do with adverts these days?" She nodded to the line of adverts that ran between the window opposite and the ceiling. She continued talking but her words went unheeded as Mary and Patrick looked up at the adverts and their hearts missed a beat.

Instead of a line of insurance adverts, they were looking at a row of messages, or rather one message spread across each frame. The words shimmered as though they were a mirage; they read:

'Hello Mary! You will be receiving some strange messages from me. Do not be alarmed as I just want to make contact with you.'

The woman's words at last registered in their brains. "Whoever this Mary is must be a lucky girl! To think that an admirer has gone to the trouble and expense of placing this message. It's very romantic!"

Mary had seen the notice before the woman spoke; perhaps her own name caught her attention and she was white faced and didn't reply. Patrick managed to give a nervous smile and stammered, "I – I think it's fascinating!"

For the rest of the journey they avoided looking at the message but had to endure to the plump woman's description of romantic fantasies from her younger days that may or may not have been true.

Needless to say, it was a sombre couple who entered the theatre. Mary immediately went to the rest room while Patrick sorted out the tickets. Despite their initial mood, the musical cheered them to some extent. They avoided the bus and took a taxi home afterwards.

Patrick immediately made some strong coffee laced with a portion of rum and they settled down to talk. At first it was banal comments, as though afraid to talk about what was really on their minds.

"I really enjoyed the play," Patrick commented.

Mary nodded, "I've always been a fan of Abba since I was a small girl. It was a good story, a bit like a French farce!"

Patrick nodded slightly, "Yes, highly improbable but very entertaining!"

"What about the notice?" Mary could no longer contain herself.

Patrick paused before answering, "It was a hell of a shock!"

"So you think that it was a message for me?" Mary could still not accept the situation.

"Oh yeah! We left from the same bus stop that you use to go to work and they must know that. It does confirm that the things we are seeing are attempts to contact you, which was plain in the message. The real questions are who, and how, and what are their intentions?"

"Did you notice that it was the clearest image we have had so far? A bit wobbly but it was clear." Mary sounded as though she was struggling with her sanity.

Patrick held up a finger, "Did you also notice that it said, 'you will be having messages,' nothing about having already sent some!"

"That doesn't make sense, unless it *was* a message from someone's beau. Perhaps we're making too much of this!" Mary sounded hopeful.

"I don't think so!" Patrick said firmly, "The advertising industry has some clever ways of pushing their message across but I've never heard or seen this before, in any case, I looked as we got off and it had disappeared."

Mary looked at her companion with a puzzled expression, "But it is all nonsense! For weeks there have been odd things happening, so surely this message, the warning should have come first!"

"That's just as odd as everything else; none of it makes sense!" Patrick confirmed.

"I feel like Alice!" Mary shook her head and looked at Patrick curiously, "I'm beginning to suspect that you're the White Rabbit or the Cheshire cat and that very soon a caterpillar will appear!"

Patrick chuckled, "I think that there is a strong possibility of Tweedledum and Tweedledee appearing; I think that it would be just the sort of nonsense that would appeal to them!"

"If we assume that everything is connected and that someone is trying to contact me, why? It's an awful lot of trouble and confusion. Wouldn't it be easier to send a message by post? They obviously can form words and wouldn't it be simpler to do that on paper?" Mary's voice had settled to one of puzzlement.

"We would think so but what if they don't have paper or the means to put the message on paper? For the want of a pen, the words were lost!"

"Very poetic! There's a flaw in that reasoning; they don't have a pen or paper but can use very high technology! That does not make sense!" Mary emphasised her words and her frustration by clutching at empty air.

"The only person who can answer those questions is the person who is trying to contact you." Patrick decided, "We will have to sit tight until he makes a better effort!"

CHAPTER FOURTEEN

Patrick blinked his eyes open; something had disturbed his sleep and he looked around the darkened living room, half expecting that there was another apparition. Then he heard a muffled cry followed by mumbling. Mary was having a dream!

He tiptoed to her bedroom and peeked around the door. She had kicked her duvet off the bed and her legs and arms were moving in tiny, nervous jerks. He walked to the bed and lifted the duvet from the floor. Very gently he recovered her but even that startled her awake; her eyes flew open and she gave a little scream as she saw the shadowed figure bending over her.

"You were having one hell of a nightmare!" Patrick calmed her down.

Recognising his voice, her head slumped back into the pillow. "Was I? Oh yeah, I remember now; I was being chased by giant eyes and mouths and everything was like being under water, even my running was slowed down!"

"You kicked off your duvet," Patrick sat down on a wicker chair next to the bed, "I covered you up and that woke you; sorry! Do you want to talk?"

"Don't apologise, it was awful!" Mary took a couple of deep breaths, "There was a lot more but I can't recall it."

"Don't worry; you were just releasing anxieties caused by our friends, if we can call them that. I'm wide awake now and thinking of making some tea; would you like some?"

"Yes please! I need to relax. Go ahead and I'll catch up."

Mary used the bathroom and joined him on the sofa. "Oh, thanks for the tea. I hope that we can solve this 'cos I can't keep having nightmares!"

"I think that we have to go on trust for the moment," Patrick stirred his tea, "It has said that it means no harm and we have to accept that for the moment."

"It's like being stalked and in a very frightening way!" Mary pulled a face, "I would be terrified if it was 'phone calls or somebody walking behind me, but this is way beyond that! Sending messages on buses is so bizarre!"

"At least it looked almost normal; the woman next to me thought it was romantic and not very unusual." Patrick paused, "What puzzles me is the sequence of the events; it's as though we were reading a book by flipping backwards and forwards."

"Have you any idea of who could be doing this?" Mary rubbed the sleep from her eyes.

Patrick shook his head but he pursed his lips in thought, "It is possible that someone is using an experimental device and that's why the results are so startling; perhaps they are having trouble with the controls."

"But why don't they just ask me by using a letter?" Mary said bitterly.

"I have no idea except what I said earlier that they don't have the normal means of communication. It's certainly intrusive but I can't see that going to the police will achieve anything." Patrick concluded.

"We have the recordings; surely seeing it on film will prove what we say!"

"Sorry, that will not be enough!" Patrick patted her arm, "They will initially think that it's something we've been playing with, a hoax and if they do accept our story the first thing they will do is send the recordings away to be analysed and that takes time. Remember all of those photographs of UFOs? They were nearly all proved to be jokes. We'll get to the bottom of it faster if we let it run its course."

"Although I see the sense of what you're saying, it doesn't stop me from feeling scared and vulnerable!" Mary brought her knees up and huddled at the end of the sofa.

CHAPTER FIFTEEN

The voice reminded Patrick of one from a distant radio, fading in and out and accompanied with crackles, whistles, and static. At first it was just a noise, associated with the appearance of a twisted face, not that it looked like a normal face; at times the jaw disappeared completely!

The apparition had made another appearance and Mary sat clutching the arms of the chair in a white knuckled embrace. It was obvious to Patrick that these appearances were becoming too much for her.

At some point the shimmering, twisting face uttered the words, "Mary", buzz, whistle, "we are trying to make contact," whistle, "difficult." The mouth kept moving, twisting out of shape but no other words could be made out through the interference.

"Well, that answers something!" Patrick said, after the image and sound had disappeared, "I think it is someone trying a new system of broadcast."

"I know no one who is capable of doing such a thing and it knows my name!" Mary said with some anger.

"But now messages are coming through and that means that they are improving the technology. In a while, we will find out exactly who it is and why they are trying to contact you."

If it were not for the presence of Patrick, Mary would have moved out. At night, he could hear her dreaming, a mumble coming from the partly opened door to her room. She had started to stay at work for longer hours, trying to escape for a while at least.

"Now my dear," Old Priestly took her aside, "You look very ill to me and I notice that you stay on for hours in the evening. You must rest, there's nothing that important, so go home and rest." Mary could not think of a reply, not one that would have made sense to the old man.

While Mary was working, Patrick played back the recordings, trying to make out more words, but the distortion was too great. A week later came a new word, "Portal." Mary was still at work and the image came while he was reading.

"I think that I begin to understand a little," Patrick informed her when she returned, "the word 'portal' must refer to a specific gap or something in the wavelengths. They are obviously trying to improve that gap."

"I don't care!" She angrily threw herself into the armchair.

"But they are improving and I think that eventually, very soon, we will get the complete message."

The buzzing noise alerted them a few nights later. Mary had just left the room to go to bed and she crept back in.

It was the same face, not exactly masculine or feminine and it was grey but the features didn't keep disappearing and the voice was much clearer.

"We have been trying to make contact for a long time. The portal keeps shifting and the problem has been to locate it and keep a steady transmission. We can hear you, if you want to speak."

"Who are you? Why do you want to talk to us?" Mary burst out, tears threatening to pour down her cheeks.

"I don't think that you would understand my name, let us say that it is Charlie. We have been looking at your world for many years and we have wanted to talk to you but only now has the device been able to enter the portal."

"Why have you been looking at me?" Mary was fighting her emotions. "You do realise that what you are doing is an intrusion and frightening us?"

"We have looked at many people, where we can. It is where our worlds converge." There was no inflection in the cold, grey voice.

Patrick's blood ran cold, "What do you mean by 'our worlds'?"

"Ah, that is quite a long explanation," the shimmering grey face replied, "We do not share the same time and space as you!"

CHAPTER SIXTEEN

It took only a few seconds for the words to sink in but to both Mary and Patrick, it seemed like hours.

"Wh – what do you mean by that," Patrick asked, "You're here, so you must be in the same time and space!"

"Only briefly," the face that called itself Charlie replied, "and I am not really with you even now!" The voice was hollow, like somebody talking through a long tube.

"What are you?" Mary asked in a small, timid voice.

"Ah, that is a big problem! "Said the hollow voice, "As we understand your language, I would be, as you would say, an alien!"

Again, the seconds seemed like hours but before they could speak Charlie continued. "As I said earlier, Charlie is not my name, nor is this my voice or even my body. There are some insurmountable barriers that prevent anything that is really me to exist in your world."

"What planet do you come from?" Mary managed to say.

Charlie gave a short laugh, "That would be difficult for you to pronounce and there is no suitable word in your language; we could say that I come from Earth!"

Mary shook her head, "I don't get it! You said that you come from a different time and space and that you cannot exist in our world, but you come from Earth. You are nuts!"

The grey face was not fazed by her comment, "Some remarkably clever people in your world have thought of something they call M-Theory. We were surprised that they could think of something that they could not see or touch or smell or even prove, but they were amazingly near the truth."

"I have read a little of this," Patrick said, "Our universe is on something like a membrane and they speculate that other universes are on other membranes."

"You have put it very well in a very few words," Charlie positively smiled, although it was twisted and would have been better if he had not, "The membrane has only two dimensions, length and breadth but no thickness so it is invisible, but it does have the T dimension – time. As far as we know, all of the membranes have time. May I ask a question?"

"Yeah, sure," Patrick said.

"We have been trying for a very long time to make contact with your world. What have you experienced of this until now?"

Patrick looked at Mary, "It was Mary that had the initial contact, perhaps she should tell you."

"The first thing that I noticed was a small, green speck of light at the corner of my eye." Mary thought back at the chain of events, "I thought that it was eye-strain but then more specks arrived, so then I thought that there must be something much more serious and a saw a doctor. Then one evening a disembodied finger appeared to be reading the same book. I threw a fit and I went on holiday where I met Patrick and he came back to help me find an answer." Mary took a deep breath, "Then both of us saw clouds of lights moving around and they seemed attracted to us."

Patrick jumped in, "I recorded some of the events and there were different shapes at different wavelengths."

Charlie nodded, as if to say that he understood but he said nothing. The movement made his head morph slightly.

Mary continued, "The next appearance was shocking, it was a shower of light pouring into the room and a buzzing noise. The next was a gigantic head with my face. I felt disgusted! The next appearance was a head but the face parts were all over the place."

"Then we got a weird sort of message while sitting on a bus, among the advertisements," Patrick took up the tale, "Then when Mary was out, I had a distorted message containing the word 'portal'. Then here you are now!"

"Yes indeed, here I am at last!" Charlie said, "I must apologise for it must have been very confusing and frightening. The problem is that your membrane and ours are not synchronised, in other words the sequence of events that you have experienced is not the same sequence that happened here."

Mary looked puzzled, "I don't understand."

"Think of a membrane as a sheet of material that ripples and flows like the sea. When our ripple is close to your membrane we can make contact, but our ripple will move along your membrane, backwards and forwards so that we see your world at different times but not in a logical sequence."

Light dawned in Patrick's head, "I see, each time your ripple comes near us will be a different time in our history, you will see at one time the Second World War and the next will be the Battle of Hastings and the next could be something in our future."

"That's it, whatever those events are, in a simplified form," Charlie confirmed, "The space in which the membranes move is not the same as space as you know it. Your concept of distance does not exist here, so being near to each other is something difficult to explain."

"You said that you could see us," Mary's head was spinning with thoughts of non-distance.

"We can see and hear you, or rather we can sense where you are and the vibrations you call sound and on those occasions when we are near, but you cannot see and hear us," Charlie explained, "The matter that makes up our world is different and your physical laws are not compatible, that is why you cannot see us. Our problem was that we were aware of you but there was no way to make our presence known to you until recently."

"So how are you making contact now?" Patrick asked.

Charlie managed a small hollow laugh, "Obviously, with some difficulty! The first problem was to lock on to a certain time and place. Unfortunately, we could not choose at that time and it turned out to be your apartment. The second problem was to use your matter to make an image, since you cannot see anything we send and that explains all of the strange events you have experienced. Again, I can only apologise for disturbing you in an alarming fashion."

"You used what we call photons. Why was that?" Patrick asked.

"Photons are a basic particle that carries energy. We have our form of photons which are very similar to yours; it was a lot easier to use those than anything else but as you have witnessed, it is not an easy thing to do." Charlie almost sounded apologetic.

"Now that you have managed to make contact, intelligible contact, will you be here for ever?" Mary asked, uncomfortable with the thought.

"No! We cannot maintain contact when the membranes drift apart," Charlie said, "We have used our technology to hold this state for as long as we can but very soon the separation will be too great to overcome; perhaps in our future we will develop better methods and technology."

"How long will you stay now?" Mary continued.

"Not very long." Charlie's face reproduced an apologetic smile.

Patrick hunched forward, "We have stories here about ghosts and people hearing voices. Is that anything to do with you?"

Charlie's face froze for a moment before replying, "It is possible that some of those stories were created from some of our efforts. We had to learn your language and it kept changing every time we managed to hear. Why do you have many different languages?"

"That's a long story!" Patrick avoided the long explanation, "Does that mean that you only have one language?"

"Yes, it makes life easier," Charlie said, "During our early attempts we wondered if it was the same place, perhaps a different world or even a different membrane. It must cause you a lot of problems!"

Patrick nodded, "It has and still does!"

"We only see glimpses of your world and so much of your history remains unknown to us. That is why we were reading your book; it was historical and interested us."

"You said that you have seen our past and our future," Mary began to understand what Charlie had been saying and picked up on this curious aspect, "Have you seen what happens in our future?"

Charlie's face froze again but for a longer period. It shimmered and went slightly out of focus before he resumed talking, "We have seen the end of your world, when your sun dies, but that is a long way into your future. Other things we have seen but we have a rule that covers this question, in that no one should see their own future. As for the lives of individuals, the same applies but it is even more difficult as we only see moments here and there. I can assure you that we have no idea of what happens to you both but I can only be sure of that from my present, perhaps in both of our futures, we will meet again."

"From your past, can you tell us if these weird events will continue in our future?" Patrick asked.

"There are a few more, I am not certain of how many but you will now know what they are and they will not be too disturbing."

"I love history," Mary began to form her question, "Have you seen things like our Jesus Christ or the very start of our civilisation?"

"Indeed, we have seen many of your epochs, but we could not make much sense of what is happening. We are aware of the importance to Jesus in your society but what we have seen of that time does not mark out any individual; there were so many that were executed and we certainly did not see any God-like manifestations. We have witnessed the Trojan Wars and your books are fairly accurate. As to the birth of your civilisation, you must understand that there were very few humans, a huge amount of animals and dense vegetation; seeing what actually took place, what we understand you would call the eureka moment, has never been observed."

Charlie's face began to break up; the grey face became individual specks of light, it went out of focus, and his voice became more distant, echoing faintly down the hollow tube. "We are losing control as the membranes move further apart. I wish you well and hope to see you again."

With that, Charlie's face dissolved and fled back to the origin, high in the corner of the room.

Mary and Patrick sat silently, lost in their thoughts.

CHAPTER SEVENTEEN

Without saying a word, Patrick stood up and went into the kitchen to make some coffee. When he returned with two steaming mugs, Mary had not moved, leaning forward with her elbows on her knees and a face lost in thought.

"What do you think of our strange visitor?" He placed the mug on the coffee table but she made no sign that she even noticed.

"I still think that it is an intrusion but I can understand why it happened, if it is true!" Her voice was quiet, so quiet that Patrick could hardly hear, then she spoke normally, "What proof have we that what he said were true?"

"None! I would point out that Charlie's explanation of the weird things that have happened here does fit the facts." Patrick said emphatically.

Mary lifted her head and stared into his face, "I would have laughed if he had said he was a Martian, but a creature from somewhere outside of the universe! I still think that it is from someone on this planet and in this time and space. He even looks human!"

"His explanation is plausible," Patrick stared back into her face, "I believe that there are aliens somewhere out there, there must be something among all of those stars and galaxies. I just never thought of anything beyond our universe."

"I always put the thoughts of aliens, little green men and flying saucers in the same category as God and the devil, or even the tooth fairy!" Mary tried to inject some humour into the conversation.

"Didn't your dad ever play Santa Claus?" Patrick caught on to a slim chance to turn her mood.

Mary smiled, "Of course he did, all fathers do that but there comes a time when you realise that reindeer don't fly!"

"But there are stars and planets and galaxies out there, you must believe in that," Patrick argued, "and there must be life on many of them and some of those will be intelligent."

"If he had said that he was from a planet that circled…" Mary waved her arms around as she tried to think of a star, "the Pole Star, there would be a chance someday that we could get there and verify the facts, but Charlie is from some mythical place that we can never reach, a real Never-Never Land! It could easily be a hoax because of that!"

"I can't disagree with that but I can suggest that the next time he appears we ask him for some proof." Patrick took a long swallow of his coffee.

CHAPTER EIGHTEEN

Mary and Patrick had some peace for a while. As the days went by and there was no reappearance of Charlie and the specks of light, the tension left the pair and life regained a semblance of normality.

It was some time before Mary wanted to discuss what had happened, but as her nerves calmed down she broached the subject.

"Can you explain what Charlie was on about? I know nothing of this membrane business and I can't believe a word of it!"

Patrick gathered his thoughts before answering, "It is all theory and mathematics, at least up until now. Basically it is all about the Big Bang and how things became as they are. When Albert Einstein described the universe it opened up a completely new line of thinking and Max Planck introduced the idea of a quantum universe."

"I've heard of these things but never really understood them," Mary admitted.

"Not everyone agrees with what is suggested and there are many variations," Patrick continued, "many different opinions, which is why you probably don't understand; I don't fully understand! Einstein spent the rest of his life trying to find the Theory of Everything, a simple explanation of the reality we experience. What it boils down to is that matter does not really exist, it is only different forms of energy. These energies have been described as tiny strings that vibrate at different frequencies; that is String Theory. A development of that idea is M-theory where all of the strings are attached to a membrane and a further development is that there is more than one membrane."

"But we can't see our membrane, or Charlie's!" Mary looked perplexed.

"It is all in mathematics, solutions to different aspects of our reality. We can't see an atom but we know that they exist; we can't see an electron but we use them daily and photons stream out of the sun in billions! All of these things were at some time just theories and mathematical expressions but experiments since then have proved their existence. It would appear that M-theory has just been proved!"

"If it is true!" Mary mumbled and then in a louder voice, "What Charlie was saying, that he has trouble creating an image here, does that mean that they don't have – thingies – in his world?"

"He probably does not have the same thingies, as you call them. I suspect that the natural laws are different but similar and that his atoms and stuff operate in a different way. I also think that Charlie is not a single person; it's an image created by a group of people."

Mary shuddered, "It's like having no walls and everyone able to see everything you do!"

"That may not be the case!" Patrick surprised her, "You're thinking that their senses operate the same way as ours but if their natural laws and their energies work differently, their seeing abilities will be something we can't imagine."

Mary looked thoughtful, "I read recently that some birds can see lines of magnetism; is that what you mean?"

"Something like that!" Patrick nodded, "Vision is simply the way our eyes receive photons, energy and the way our brains use that signal. Perhaps Charlie senses us in a totally different way."

"I'm not sure that makes me any more comfortable! It's still an invasion of my, our privacy!" Mary slumped in the chair.

"What we need is a permanent contact," Patrick declared, "You heard that they cannot determine exactly when they make contact but if we could anchor the signal we could arrange certain times. The other thing is that our scientists could gain a huge amount from a permanent contact; think of all of the science that we could exchange!"

Mary looked up and stared directly into Patrick's eyes, "He said that we had thought about the M-theory so he has been looking elsewhere. Why haven't we heard about that?"

"Think back, when you first saw the specks you thought that there was something medically wrong with you. Perhaps the other people also thought the same and said nothing."

CHAPTER NINETEEN

Mary started to search the Internet, looking for articles about String Theory and M-theory. Normally she would never have even thought of doing that; her interests lay elsewhere but the present situation had changed that.

Not until she had got the ideas firmly in her head or at least as best one could for something so way out, did she tell Patrick what she had been doing.

He looked at her, "And what do you think?"

"I think that it is impossible! Then I think about the specks of light, the hand and the faces and that confuses me; I can't relate those images to these theories!"

Patrick nodded, "You have dived into the deep end so I'm not surprised that you are confused. These are the result of many things coming together over a long period of time. Up until nineteen hundred it was thought that the universe was static and ticked along like a big clock. Then Max Planck suggested energy came in the form of quanta, little packets. No one believed him, even Einstein but Einstein used the theory to produce some theories of his own, the most famous of these was how the universe really was. He was in doubt about his own theories as his calculations said that the universe was expanding, so he inserted a constant to keep the universe as it had been thought of for thousands of years. He said that it was his biggest mistake because shortly afterwards someone else found that the universe was really expanding. Einstein removed the constant!"

"Einstein got it wrong!" Mary's eyebrows arched upward in surprise.

"Only in detail, basically he has been proved correct many times and those theories have been expanded to where we are today. Long before Einstein, mathematicians had been working on the idea of more dimensions than those we experience and that attracted the curious; they asked why would that appear in calculations without it being a reality?"

Mary gave a disbelieving, scoffing laugh, "If that happened at work, we would think that there was an error in the calculations and we would be right!"

"Many thought exactly that but the interesting thing was that without the references to other dimensions nothing worked! I am talking about things that we can observe and know are correct. Without those other dimensions the world would not exist and nor could you and I!" Patrick wagged a finger at her.

That left Mary in a thoughtful state. She was grappling with these strange, impossible ideas, while at the same time there were the images that both of them had seen, proof that there were some strange realities. She was really glad that she had invited Patrick on a whim or she would have really thought that she had gone mad!

Two days went by as she mulled over these thoughts and her emotions. The events had left her uncertain, uncertain in the everyday things; was the bus that she caught to work really there? Were the people she passed actually real human beings? All of the papers that she dealt with daily, were they appertaining to real people and places? Was the great face that talked to them the actual reality?

The one thing that she didn't feel any more was being scared. That surprised her! When the lights first appeared she was horror stricken that she might have a brain tumour but this fantastic, awesome, speaking face she was not afraid of. Normally, she should have been terrified!

Her mind still in a whirlwind of thoughts and ideas she sat down one evening to talk about them. "In the broadest terms, how would you describe what is happening to these two membranes?"

They had eaten a meal and sat as usual, waiting to see if anything appeared. Patrick sipped at his hot coffee as he thought out the reply.

"Well, the first thing is that there may be more than two! That is just a side issue and it can never be proved unless they make contact. As I can visualise it, the two membranes move separately in something that is not space and time; space and time only exist within the membranes and that also means that those things may not be the same. Time is a condition of entropy, where things wear out and lose energy. I wouldn't think that the energy dissipation would be the same in both places. As to the spatial dimensions, I have no idea!"

"That's one of the things I've been trying to understand," Mary screwed her face up in a frown, "Charlie said that he could see us but why can't we see them, the real them?"

"Charlie said that they cannot exist in our world. I would take that to mean that their atoms, or what we think of as atoms are entirely different and don't correspond to the physical laws that we have. There are suggestions that what we think are real, at the very minute level of laws and energies, may not be real. If their laws were the same as ours, we could see them."

"I wonder what they really look like," Mary said in her little girl's voice; a thoughtful little voice.

"I don't think we can comprehend their physical appearance; it must be far beyond anything we can ever imagine! There is also their timing to think about. Charlie sent several images which to him were in a normal linear time but they came here out of a sequence. I can imagine that these membranes are waving around, like seaweed in the tide, so that the two membranes touch at different times both here and there. I also suspect that at different places on both membranes."

"It must be just as confusing for them as well!" Mary exclaimed with a sudden realisation.

"Probably not as much as they are conducting the experiment but it must mean that they will have appeared to many people at different times; think of all of the holy visions, ghosts, and other odd reports. At least some of them could have been Charlie and his friends."

Mary had a thought, "Are you saying that Joan of Arc really did hear voices?"

Patrick shrugged his shoulders, "I'm not saying anything, just a maybe. What about the UFO sightings, a few were never properly explained. I also think that there are a lot of people locked away because of Charlie's experiment!"

"What an awful thought!" Mary's eyes flew wide open, "What does that make Charlie, a monster or some mindless, mad doctor?"

"You're thinking in human terms; there is no reason to suppose that their morals or laws are the same as ours. It stands to reason that if their physical properties, the atoms are different, then everything else would be."

"We don't really know what we're dealing with and is it safe to continue? I'm starting to get the shudders!" Her faced puckered up.

"We know that he or they are intelligent," Patrick tried to calm her down, "He knew that he had startled us but perhaps that does not go as far as realising that they have placed people in a difficult situation. All we can do is to find out more and educate them."

CHAPTER TWENTY

"I've got to make a move," Patrick announced over breakfast, "I have to get some work and I have to pay the rent on my apartment shortly. What worries me is how you will be without company."

Mary took a sip of coffee as she thought over his statement and finally she set the cup down, "I was wondering how long you would stay. Obviously you're using up money and you need a job. I can't say that I feel comfortable meeting Charlie by myself; I know that it is just an image but there may be other things that we haven't seen yet."

"I can look for some work more locally than Manchester. I have a few contacts that may provide something. That just leaves where I'm going to live," Patrick looked at Mary with a question written all over his face.

Clare took another sip of coffee before answering, "I think that you could stay here but we would have to improve your sleeping arrangements."

"The only problem there is that I have a heap of stuff that would fill this place and then some!" Patrick informed her.

Mary thought for a moment, "Let me have a word with the landlord; there may be a place near here. At least it could house all of your rubbish." Her mouth twitched almost in laughter at the tease.

"It's not rubbish! It is highly technical trash!" Patrick caught her barb and smiled, "That's solved then! I need to give a month's notice and that will give us some time to look for somewhere. Today, I will make a few 'phone calls and knock on a few doors."

Mary had been wondering how long the present situation could last. Obviously he had his own life to lead and she was grateful that he had spent so much time on her problem. She had become accustomed to having a flat-mate and he was an amusing, humorous companion and very supportive. If it would become something else, she was unsure of.

Patrick arrived fairly late that evening. It was obvious that he had a few drinks but he was not falling down, not quite, and had a huge smile on his face.

"Got it! Done it! Been there! You are looking at the latest college lecturer at the polytechnic!" He bowed deeply and nearly fell over!

Mary's response was to smile at his condition and at the good news, "What are you going to teach?"

"Photography of course! For the rest of this term they are taking me on as a supernumerary, but next term I will get a full contract." He had more than a little problem in pronouncing supernumerary.

"And you have been celebrating!" Mary observed.

"Hmm, it's not what you know but who you know!" Patrick sat down heavily in the armchair, he almost collapsed into it, "Johnny Pinner was at college with me and he has got himself into the local education board. A few calls from him and there was a genuine vacancy, and with his endorsement I got the job! Went to his place, lovely wife, had dinner there and then finished off in the pub. Missed me?"

Mary was laughing, "You do realise that your performance is being recorded?"

Patrick stared blearily at the camera with its blinking red light, "Oh bother!"

"I had words with the landlord and she thinks that there is a chance of an apartment in this block," Mary gave him more news, "She said that she will tell us tomorrow." But she was talking to herself, as a loud snore had emerged from Patrick.

She placed a blanket over him and stood for a moment, studying him and wondered what she had let herself in for!

In the morning Patrick looked suitably shattered. Sleeping in the armchair hadn't helped! He gulped down coffee at a fast rate, helping himself to a second cup.

"When do you start this job?" Mary asked, partly amused and partly scornful.

"Monday, thank God! I don't think that I could face a classroom full of eager students at the moment! The present lecturer will show me the ropes before I dive in the deep end. Did I hear you say that there is an apartment?"

"Maybe, I'll get a confirmation later today. Charlie appeared last night, or at least that noise and the lights. Only for about ten minutes and nothing else."

"Hmm, you appear okay with that!" Patrick made an observation as well as asking a question.

"I think that knowing, at least in partly knowing, helps in accepting what is happening. My hair still stands up when it happens!" Mary gave a twisted grin.

She went to work, leaving her companion making another pot of fresh coffee.

On the Saturday, she went with him in his battered Ford to Manchester. Confirmation of the apartment in the same block as hers had come through, so now they were cancelling the contract in Manchester and assessing what Patrick would bring back or throw away.

Before she could climb in the Ford, Patrick cleared some items from the front seat. She eyed the rest of the estate car; it was full of tripods, camera cases, and other things she could not identify. It wasn't so much untidy, it was just full!

He apologised, "I'm sorry about this but I can never be sure of what I will be doing, so a take as much as possible."

"Well, you've cluttered up my apartment, so I should expect that you do the same to your car!" Mary climbed in and they set off.

Patrick's apartment was in an old building and it was on the fourth floor. Mary noticed that there was no lift and wondered how much Patrick was going to carry down the stairs. She soon found out! The living room doubled as a studio and was the only clear space in the apartment.

Mary walked from room to room, or at least as far as the doors and peeked inside. One room was obviously a darkroom; the windows covered in black cloth and trays stood on benches. There were two enlargers, or what she took to be enlargers but there were other machines that she had no idea of their function.

Patrick looked embarrassed, "I've been here for about ten years and I just accumulated stuff as I needed it. Now I see that it will be a problem!"

"I don't know anything about the technical stuff, that's your department, but you will need furniture; a bed, table and chairs, a sofa, armchairs, and everything in the kitchen," Mary ticked off the items on her fingers, "You do have these things?"

"Um, er, I think so! I was here so seldom that I can't remember. Underneath all of this I suppose." Patrick scratched his head.

"If I were you, I would get boxes and pack everything in them and then hire a firm to do the moving. This will take you more than a month and running back and forth will cost a fortune!"

Patrick had to agree, "I will only have weekends anyway, so that means just the packing."

Mary took pity on him, "I'll give you a hand; that should speed things up!"

She looked at Patrick and saw that he was looking past her with his mouth off latch. She turned and saw a small ball of lights spinning in the hall. Her blood ran cold; the last thing she expected to see was Charlie!

CHAPTER TWENTY-ONE

As they looked, it vanished!

"W – what was that doing here?" Patrick stuttered, "I thought that Charlie could only appear in your place!"

"Obviously not, since he's here!" Mary's voice had a slight tremble, revealing that she was only just controlling her surprise.

"Was it a stray occurrence and nothing to do with what is happening at your place?" Patrick wondered.

Mary shook her head, "Who knows? Something we can ask when we see him again," she took a deep breath, "Concentrate on the here and now! Shall we go and get some boxes and then we can start packing?"

Patrick continued looking at where the lights had appeared, his mind racing with thoughts, "I think that they're improving their control; now they can trace us where ever we are!"

"Is that a good thing?" Mary asked.

"Dunno! It might be if Charlie can pick the location and time rather than these haphazard appearances."

Mary shuddered, "I wish they would stop completely!"

Over the next few weeks they managed to box everything and the few items that wasn't boxed they brought back in Patrick's Ford. Mary insisted that the new apartment should be cleaned and a team of professionals were brought in to do that. Then she bought new curtains and some cans of paint.

"We can at least brighten up the walls and woodwork, it doesn't look as though they've been touched for some time!" She paused for a moment and then took a brush and painted a huge face on the wall. "If we leave that, perhaps it will frighten Charlie away!"

"I have a feeling that Charlie can't be frightened," Patrick took a different colour and turned the sombre face into that of a clown.

Patrick's work at the polytechnic proved to be pleasurable. The staff accepted him warmly, the facilities were excellent and the work not too arduous. He realised that he would not have to set up a darkroom at home as he could use one of those in the polytechnic.

He did have one problem in that although he knew what he was doing, he had to explain to the students. It was some years since he had studied the subject and he had to do some homework to recall the precise terms. Technology had also moved on and it was less about chemistry and more about electronics.

After he had moved into the new apartment, which still looked as though it was a storage space with the boxes only partly unpacked, he took to staying on after classes for an hour or two and using the darkroom.

It was there that Charlie appeared once more. Patrick was transferring film from the camera to the developing drum and all of the lights were extinguished. He became aware of the familiar buzz and a short time after a few sparks of light appeared and slowly grew. Thankfully, the film was in the drum and not exposed to the light.

This was quite novel, as this was the first time he had seen the lights in complete darkness. They appeared to be much brighter, bright enough for him to see the room clearly with its reflecting surfaces and deep shadows. Also, these lights did not burst violently outwards; they gradually built up until Charlie's face appeared.

"Hi Charlie, you've made some changes!" he greeted the face that did not distort as before. It floated solidly at about Patrick's height.

The grey lips parted, "Hello Patrick, you are correct! Are they that obvious?" Even the voice sounded firmer.

Patrick nodded, "Oh Yeah! You have increased control of the equipment and now it is not so alarming. You have also learned to track a target."

"That sounds very aggressive – a target!" Charlie managed to pull an expression of distaste, "I would prefer a point of interest but you are correct in that too; most of the time we can now locate you."

"Mary is not with me, which is probably a good thing!" Patrick grunted.

"So we understand, which is why we, I want to talk to you alone." Charlie sounded serious.

Patrick nodded again, "Well, it's not surprising that she is distressed! You invade people's privacy and some of your displays have been horrifying!"

"Yes, I apologise for that! You do not seem to be as distressed as Mary and that interests us." As Charlie spoke there were slight hesitations before some words, as though he was searching for the right ones.

Patrick nodded, "We are all different and we react in various ways to what we experience. Mary has had a fairly sheltered life, just school and working in a quiet office. I on the other hand have been in some very difficult and noisy places, so I'm more used to surprises."

"You are individuals?" Charlie's voice sounded surprised and interested.

Patrick wasn't sure if that was a question or a statement. "Of course we are!"

"We find the idea of individual entities and privacy most peculiar! We know the words and their meaning as far as you are concerned but to us they are strange concepts!"

"You're not individuals?" Patrick sounded surprised and more than a little puzzled.

There was a hesitation, "Not in the way that you are! You have private thoughts and some prefer to live alone in those thoughts and most only in small groups and yet perversely you huddle in vast communities."

"You mean cities?" Patrick started to get some idea of what he was talking to, "We do that because we are more efficient in what we do, rather than as isolated groups or individuals. How do you live?"

"As one!"

Patrick was stumped at that answer and sought clarification, "You can understand what each of you are thinking?"

"Of course! Even that is difficult for us to comprehend; until we met individuals we didn't have any idea that life could be that different. The idea that there could be others, individuals is alien to us!" Patrick smiled at the idea that he was alien. "So you know what each other is thinking and there are no surprises! We are always being surprised and that is why we fear things and have phobias."

"We have no fear!" The calm statement was unsettling.

Again, Patrick was surprised at the answer and stumped once more.

Charlie continued, "We have noted these words you use, fear, shock, horror, disgust and surprise. Until we met you we had never really experienced surprise and even with you it is more of just a curiosity."

"Surely things can happen that you have no contact with?" Patrick tried to think of an example, "What if a meteor strikes you from outer space? That would be a surprise that would bring fear and horror!"

For the first time the grey face smiled, displaying a set of grey teeth, "Your ideas of space and time do not correspond to ours. There are no things that you call meteors. Even now after meeting you, we have difficulty in understanding that you can and have to travel distances. We have a form of distance but we have no need to travel!"

"I cannot visualise that!" Patrick was baffled.

"And I cannot explain it in terms that you would understand!" Charlie replied.

"What about life and death?" Patrick tried another line of thought.

"'I think, therefore I am', is that not what one of your philosophers once said? When we first emerged from the chaos of creation, yes, we were created from the same source as yourselves, we have existed. We evolve, change and develop but we do not die!"

Patrick was shattered! He felt his blood tingling coldly in his veins, "D – do you mean that you're immortal?"

"We do not know and we will not until the end of time!" The calmness of the voice was as disturbing as the message.

Patrick was startled by a knocking on the door of the darkroom.

"Sir, it's the janitor. We're about to lock up," came the voice from outside.

"Okay, I'll be out in a moment!" The interruption had startled him back to this reality, his reality! He looked around the room and noticed that the shadows were increasing as the light faded.

"We will continue this at another time, goodnight!" Charlie said as the grey face faded into the darkness of the room.

Patrick opened the door and found the janitor waiting and waving a set of keys in his hand. "I hope I didn't interrupt you?" the janitor said and then looked enquiringly into the darkroom, "I thought you were talking to someone?"

"I-pod," Patrick patted his pocket even though he never had owned an I-pod, "The only place I can get a decent conversation!"

CHAPTER TWENTY-TWO

Mary had gone out for the evening with some of her girlfriends from college. They wanted to know where she had been, why the long silence. As soon as they heard that she had a new flat-mate and that it was a male, they thought that they understood completely. She then had to field questions about Patrick. She felt a bit uncomfortable about misleading them but they seemed happy that she had a boyfriend.

Patrick drove home in a bit of a daze, so much so that he lost concentration and became lost. Finding his bearings, he then found his parking slot and entered the apartment.

He stopped in surprise. The place was dark, just the red blinking light of the camera and then he remembered that Mary had said she was going out.

He made some tea and carried that and the biscuit tin into the living room. He sat down and thought about what he had heard from Charlie.

What sort of world did Charlie live in? A place without travelling? Perhaps he should say Charlies, as there seemed to be more than one but he said that they were one! He recalled that in an earlier conversation Charlie had said that the laws of physics as we knew them did not apply. That would explain some of the puzzle, if not in detail. And they had existed since the Big Bang and would continue to live until the universe died! That thought shook him deeply; a creature that could live for billions of years!

He decided that he needed to talk to Steven Hawking or even Steven Spielberg, but decided instead that he would find some books on far out science. The trouble was, how do you describe the books, what title or subject would produce the correct books?

After a few hours of these thoughts he grew tired. Mary had still not reappeared, so he had a shower and went to bed. His bed had been set up in the spare room and he lay there still thinking about the Charlie's universe. He heard Mary come home but decided to talk to her in the morning. Then he abruptly fell asleep!

He awoke early and realised that he had been thinking about the previous night's conversation while he slept. He felt as though he had been drinking! He lay there, trying desperately to wake fully and then rose and padded into the bathroom.

He dashed cold water onto his face and hung over the basin, trying hard to get his stuff together. As he came out of the bathroom, Mary was waiting.

"I thought that I was the one out last night; you look awful!" She exclaimed.

"Hmm, I had a troubled night. Wait until I get some coffee inside me and I'll tell you what happened." His body felt as though it belonged to someone else.

During his second cup of coffee he related all that Charlie had said.

Mary shuddered, "I'm not sure I feel any better for knowing! He actually said that they never die?"

Patrick nodded slowly, "Yup! Of course it could be all a fabrication or perhaps his, their idea of time is a lot different to ours or even their concept of death."

"Dead is dead, I didn't think there was an alternative to dying!" Mary said wryly.

Patrick shrugged, "From what he said we have to think of things differently where he is concerned. Everything we accept as normal does not appear to exist on his planet. I'm not even sure that it could be called a planet! Unfortunately we were interrupted!"

"What are you going to do?" Mary asked.

"On Saturday I am going to go to the library and see if there are any books about some way out, speculative science. I have a feeling that they will have been written by crackpots and may not help!" Patrick smiled grimly.

"Why crackpots?" Mary was amused at the thought and smiled.

"There the only ones who would dare to write such nonsense!" Patrick took another cup of coffee, "How did your evening go?"

"Well, they wanted to know why I hadn't been around and so I told them about you," she informed him.

Patrick scowled at her, "What did you tell them about me? I hope that you haven't been making up fairy stories!"

"I told them that you were a secret millionaire and that we were having a madly passionate love affair." Dimples appeared on her cheeks as she saw Patrick's shocked expression, "No, I simply said that I am living with you and they made assumptions!" Mary looked innocently at her cup, "It was a lot easier than telling them that I had been talking to aliens!"

"I can't disagree with you there!" Patrick said moodily.

"Do you know what sort of books you'll be looking for?" Mary changed the subject.

Patrick shrugged his shoulders, "I'm puzzled at what Charlie said, 'we have a sort of distance but we do not travel'. What sort of world is that? I have never had to study that sort thing, nor ever wanted to!"

Mary came to a decision, "I'll come with you to the library; two heads are better than one and it'll be faster!"

It was surprisingly faster than they thought it would be! On the Friday night they used the Internet search engines to find out what there was to find. They came across the Big Bang, black holes, wormholes, and the Dirac Sea but there was little about speculation concerning other universes. The most that they found simply said that they may exist.

When they invaded the library, it took a short time to select the books that were available. They staggered into the apartment with an armful of books each which they dumped on the coffee table.

"Do you think that the answer is somewhere in these?" Mary said as she made a large pot of coffee and Patrick made some sandwiches.

"Well, it's pretty obvious that the universe is not quite as we thought! I knew some of these things from general reading, not in detail but I had heard of them and the occasional movie. I don't think any of them can describe Charlie's world but we might get some ideas."

They settled down to reading for the afternoon, punctuated by frequent refills of the coffee-pot. Mary read quietly, turning the pages while a little crease appeared between her eyes. Patrick gave an occasional grunt over something and frequently flicking back through the pages to re-read something.

By dinnertime, Mary had finished one book and complained of a headache. Patrick was a fast reader and had started on a third book. He laid the book down and sighed.

"What do you think?" He yawned.

"Nothing at the moment! My head is still spinning! How on earth did these guys come up with these ideas?" Mary pushed the heels of her hands into her eye sockets.

"Slowly is the answer to that! Planck didn't believe that his solution to the black body problem was real and neither did anyone else. Einstein used the solution to come up with the Theory of Relativity five years later and he didn't fully believe that! Twenty years after that, Dirac pointed out that Einstein's theory suggested that there was anti-matter. It was a series of small steps in trying to understand reality."

Mary leaned back in the armchair with her eyes closed, "Reality! If I had not seen Charlie I would not have believed that anything of this could be possible!"

"There has been something that I have always wondered about," Patrick stood to relieve the stiffness in his legs, "When the Big Bang occurred the universe expanded like a balloon, but expanded into what? Everything that exists, as far as we are concerned is inside the universe, inside the balloon, so what's outside – really nothing at all?"

I don't know, I can't think at the moment!" Mary opened her eyes, "Would you like a Chinese? My treat! I need a break to digest this and I can do that while digesting some sweet and sour!"

The Chinese food must have worked! Patrick woke up in the morning to find Mary still in her dressing gown and reading intently.

"How long have you been up?" Patrick looked at the clock and was surprised that it was only six-thirty.

"I couldn't sleep! It was what you said about everything we know is contained within a boundary, a balloon. At one time in the beginning it must have all been within a very small space. Now one of these books talks about the multi-verse and it occurred to me that what if Charlie's universe didn't expand like ours. That would make a huge difference in distance and time."

Patrick rubbed the sleep out of his eyes, "I need some coffee before thinking at all! It sounds interesting but I need to wake up!"

CHAPTER TWENTY-THREE

Patrick showered and then made some coffee and toast. He laid the table and dragged Mary away from the books. She had continued reading furiously and was reluctant to stop.

"I never dreamed that anyone could think of such wonderful worlds!" she exclaimed, "I feel as though I've been blind all of my life!"

"Just take it easy!" Patrick tried to calm her down, "All of the worlds mentioned in those books are only possible worlds until they are proved! There are tantalising hints but some of the mathematics is incomplete or perhaps beyond any mathematics or experiments we could ever do."

"But that's my point! Charlie has shown that at least one of these worlds is possible!" Mary took a huge bite of toast.

"I agree with you but now we have to decide on what world and can someone explain the science and maths of that world. We need to talk to someone." Patrick frowned as he buttered some toast.

"We can ask Charlie!" Mary said brightly.

"He may not be able to explain so that we understand. I was thinking of someone in this world." Patrick nibbled at the toast.

"Who?" she asked.

"I have no idea!" Patrick waved a hand aimlessly, "We had better not start by saying we have seen an alien or they will not listen. We have to ask questions and steer them in that direction, only then could we introduce Charlie - maybe."

"We can ask one of those!" Mary pointed to the pile of books. It took a second or two before Patrick realised that she was referring to the authors and not the books themselves.

"I know for a fact that most of them have mountains of trash mail from fringe lunatics. They will be hard to contact," he argued.

"We can try after breakfast!" Mary then devoted her attention to the breakfast and even cooked some eggs.

They spent the rest of the day finding web sites of the authors and as Patrick had said, it was very difficult to access any of them but there was one.

CHAPTER TWENTY-FOUR

Professor Clive Anderson liked to spend his Sundays with his family, as most parents do. He was often absent at some conference on the other side of the world and during the week while at home his work as cosmologist entailed discussions with students and colleagues into the evenings and past his children's bedtime. Sundays were precious!

His ancient, large house on the outskirts of Fenstanton, Cambridgeshire, was an easy drive to his office in Cambridge, and yet far enough away to avoid unnecessary intrusions. His wife Rachel untidily kept the large garden but it was a peaceful retreat for thinking about the complexity of the universe.

As the family was called in by Rachel for dinner, Clive opened up his computer and checked the e-mails. This was his private e-mail address and only available to close friends, family and the faculty, so he was surprised to find a message forwarded from his office in Cambridge. Probably someone there thought that it was interesting or important enough for his attention. Who would be working there on a Sunday he wondered?

He opened the e-mail and glanced at the contents, not really paying attention and hurried into the dining room to coax his three-year old son to eat and to tease his seven-year old daughter.

The children had gone to bed and he had spent some time talking to Rachel before he returned to his study. The e-mail was still on the screen, beckoning for his attention.

It was from a M. Kingman with no indication of gender. The content concerned the nature of the universe and if and how other universes would differ. It went into some detail about if time and space could be different to our universe and if the laws of physics were so different that our particles and atoms could not exist there and their equivalent could not exist here. Finally, it asked if contact could ever be made with another universe.

He didn't reply immediately; the questions had set off thoughts in his own head. By a strange coincidence he had a mini-meeting about this exact subject just two weeks earlier. He recalled the details of the meeting. It had been a meeting of different disciplines and he was the only cosmologist present. The meeting had been called as an informal discussion concerning gravity but it had spiralled off into other directions and was continued in the pub until quiet late.

The truth was that no one knew! Equations were presented proving or disproving one brilliant theory and another but no clear conclusion could be drawn. He was strangely quiet when he re-joined his wife to watch TV, absently looking at the screen but not seeing anything.

In the morning he appeared to be his normal self; he told his daughter to be good at school and promised to read her homework when he returned. He kissed everyone goodbye and drove to his office. He greeted everyone he met, took some letters from his secretary and settled down at his desk. The original message was on his computer, silently waiting for an answer.

He should have handed it to his secretary for a standard type of answer but the questions interested him. He tapped out a reply, asking for some details about the sender, stating that it was one of the most difficult questions in science today and he wanted to send answers that would be understandable.

Mary received the answer on her machine at work when she logged in on her own address. She was stumped! Neither she nor Patrick were scientists or even students, so how seriously would he take their questions? She decided that she and Patrick would talk it over in the evening.

Patrick was firm on several points, "We can't mention Charlie or even the type of world he describes!"

"Why not? I mean about his world. We could mention that we are amateurs who just happened to come up with these ideas about other universes."

"That could work!" Patrick thought for a moment, "There are thousands of amateurs in astronomy and they are taken seriously. I think that is the line to take!"

They composed an answer and sent it that evening. Unfortunately, Anderson was at a meeting in Holland for a few days and did not receive it until he returned. Mary and Patrick began to wonder if they were being ignored.

Finally they received an invitation to meet Anderson at the Cambridge Observatory. He explained that he could better explain the answers to their questions at the observatory.

They had expected to see something like Mount Palomar in California; a huge white dome that dominated the scene. Instead they could hardly see the small domes through the trees.

They asked at the reception and were taken to Anderson's office. Anderson surprisingly turned out to be just slightly older than themselves. Mary had visions of an elderly Einstein figure; how could this young fellow know about the secrets of the universe?

Anderson greeted them warmly and even sent his secretary to fetch coffee.

"So, you're amateur astronomers?" he said as they settled down. His guests stared around the room and noticed the white-boards and bookcases and that there were no marvellous instruments, not even a telescope.

"We would like to thank you for inviting us," Mary said, "We have no idea of what we are thinking of and badly need some direction and we could be wasting your time."

Patrick shook his head, "I don't know what we are! We are new to this and we just have some questions that occurred to us from what we have been reading."

"So you haven't bought a telescope yet; that's when the questions usually start coming. But you've made the journey to Cambridge to find answers, so that means you feel that it is important. A good place to start!" Clive smiled encouragingly.

'If he only knew how important', Mary thought.

"You probably already know that everything in this area is pure theory and at the moment there is no way we can verify any of those theories." Anderson paused and received nods to confirm his statement.

Patrick interrupted, "I have wondered for a long time that if the universe expanded after the Big Bang: what was it that it had expanded into? Then we both had the idea that if there was another type of universe, where both matter and energy were different, we would not be able to see it."

"That is crudely correct but it is much more complicated than that. If the matter and energy were very different both universes could occupy the same space without being aware of each other. Is that the sort of thing you were thinking?" Clive tried to establish the true nature of the question.

"That sounds similar," Mary said, "I was reading about M-theory where two membranes exist with totally different physical properties but it was suggested that from time to time, every few billion years they could touch. What impressed me about that was that there were no limitations to the membranes, that they are two dimensional and without thickness, the two other dimensions disappearing into infinity."

Anderson smiled, "Mathematicians and scientists do not like infinities so we tend to shy away from anything that suggests infinity, mainly because it cannot be measured! However, that concerns this universe and may not be viable in another universe. The thing about membranes is that they exist outside of any universe; they support universes, the fabric which we call energy/matter, without being otherwise detectable."

"So there is no way that two universes can meet?" Patrick asked.

"Have you read 'Flatland' by Abbott?" The pair shook their heads so Anderson continued, "Abbott wrote this in the eighteen-eighties and it describes living in a two-dimensional world. In there, he describes a three-dimensional sphere that descends through Flatland. At first, all that the Flatland natives see is a spot, then it grows larger and larger and then back to a dot before vanishing. They have no idea what has happened but the important thing is that they did not see reality in the shape of a sphere; a sphere is impossible in Flatland."

"So if we saw anything from another dimension we would not see what was really there; reality?" Mary began to grasp the argument.

"Sticking to Abbott's story, is the sphere reality or is there another dimension with something else that resembles a sphere in another dimension and only a dot in yet another? It really is a conundrum since we only have experience and therefore explanations for this four-dimensional world!" Anderson steepled his fingers and smiled at them.

"And there are an infinite number of dimensions and therefore an infinite number of worlds, all with an infinite number of realities," Mary said and then smiled, "Sorry about the infinite but that was what I read!"

"Don't apologise, I am constantly coming up to infinities; can't get away from them!" Anderson said, "Even if it is not infinity it's a damn large number and a problem for anyone contemplating the question of reality."

"In the example of Flatland, the two worlds do meet!" Mary pointed out, "they do become aware of each other, it's just that there is some confusion about what is there."

Anderson nodded, "As I said at the beginning, it is a complex question. You take the example of particles, the things that make up atoms and therefore things like us. They have certain properties; a positive or negative charge, spin, other things like that. We have calculated that if any of these values alter by just a fraction, the universe could never have come into being! Everything is finely balanced and considering another type of particle in another type of universe is a little beyond us."

"Are you saying that there can be no other type of universe?" Patrick asked.

"No, far from it!" Anderson replied, "It is simply beyond our imaginations to know where and how to look, what sort of calculations should we use. Now tell me about this experience that you have had!"

CHAPTER TWENTY-FIVE

The silence was palpable! Mary and Patrick first of all stared at Anderson with wide eyes and Patrick's jaw fell open, and then they looked at each other.

Anderson laughed, "It was simple! You have just become interested in the Cosmos and yet you have not bought a telescope; you ask questions that are at the far end of any learning curve and you find this compelling enough to contact me and come to Cambridge. I surmise from this and the questions that you ask that you recently had an experience, strange enough to make you consider that another world has made contact. Am I right?"

"And you think we're nuts!" Patrick muttered.

Anderson was still laughing, "Far from it! You had an experience and you didn't jump to conclusions, you tried to find out and that was the right thing to do. Now tell me about this experience!"

Mary took a deep breath, "A few months ago I started to see specks of coloured light."

"So you experienced this first, you weren't together?" Clive twitched a finger between his guests.

Mary shook her head, "At first I thought that I may have a brain tumour but then I realised that if my eyes were closed or I was not in my apartment, there were no lights. If I had a tumour I would have seen them at anytime, anywhere. Then I saw a finger, a horrible thing where I could see the bones and sinews; it was as though it was reading the book I was reading. So I went on holiday and met Patrick, I told him my problem and he offered to help."

"You saw a finger?" Anderson blinked in astonishment. Mary just nodded, tight lipped.

Patrick took up the story, "I'm a photographer, so I set up cameras to see if I could catch these lights and I also borrowed some sensitive equipment to detect any stray radiation, changes in atmospheric density, temperature, and humidity."

Anderson leaned forward, his face now serious, "That was very thorough! Why did you do that?"

"I reasoned that if there were lights there would be changes in other things. We have all of the recordings. Well, shortly after I was in Mary's apartment the lights appeared and I got a clear shot of them."

"Then things started to get really weird!" Mary continued the story, "We had starbursts, torrents of light pouring into the room and strange noises, like buzzing. Then the face appeared!"

This time it was Anderson's jaw that dropped open, "You saw a face?"

"Several faces," Patrick saw that Mary was feeling the tension, so he continued the story, "I forget in what sequence they came but one looked remarkably like Mary! One was huge and it was melting and you could see through the skin and bone!" Patrick gave a shudder, "Others were smaller but still the same and then Charlie appeared!"

"Who is Charlie?" Anderson demanded.

"I know, it's a daft name for an alien but that's what he called himself! He said that we couldn't pronounce his real name." Patrick felt stupid and angry; he could see why no one would believe this.

"You forgot the bus!" Mary said quietly.

"Oh yeah! We went out one night and took the bus. On one of those adverts above the seats was a message for Mary, it even used her name. It said that 'they' were sending messages and that she should not be worried. Even the lady next to us saw it! As we got off I looked back and the message was gone!"

Anderson held his hand up, "Stop there a moment! First it was just Mary, then both of you and now a strange lady on a bus. This doesn't sound like the usual Close Encounters of the Third Kind! Who is Charlie?"

"I think that the buzzing noise we heard each time was them trying to send speech. Charlie is the alien, only he isn't! When they could control the transmission, even the image became normal, he told us that he could not send an image of himself and that he had made up this to look human." Patrick finished.

Anderson nodded, "I see, this is why you started reading up about other universes."

"And a lot more!" Patrick held his hands out to signify a large amount, "Charlie said that they were on something like a membrane and that when they came close to our membrane, they could make contact. That's how they learned our language and some of our history."

Mary interrupted, "He actually said that they witnessed some of our history! He said that the membranes ripple so that at first they could not control where or when they made contact. It would be interesting to hear what actually happened!"

"Did he say anything about the future?" Clive asked.

"Only that he wasn't allowed to reveal our future to us," Mary opened her hands and shrugged.

"Hmm, was that the last contact that you had?" Clive could hardly believe what they said but he was reluctant to send them away.

"No, the last one was only to me, delivered in the darkroom at the polytechnic," Patrick hunched forward, head down as he pulled the memories out of his mind, "He said that his world had distance, a sort of distance but they had no need to travel. Then he said that he could not understand some of our feelings, like fear. He couldn't understand why his transmissions were upsetting us. Finally, he said that they were immortal!"

Anderson looked very interested, "Did he actually say that he or they were immortal?"

Patrick thought for a moment, "No, when I asked him he said that he didn't know, only that they appeared shortly after creation and had existed ever since."

"That is billions of years!" murmured Anderson.

"So are we mad or is it some prank by a weirdo?" Mary asked. She was so tense that tears were showing in her eyes.

"No madder than anyone else!" Anderson smiled encouragingly at her, "I would like to meet this Charlie. Why on earth did he pick such a daft name?"

"You mean he's a proper Charlie?" Patrick chuckled, "That's the only really funny thing about any of this!"

"We don't know when he will appear but you're welcome to look at all of the recordings!" Mary offered.

"That stuff is really for the technicians, I would be happy with just the camera recordings. You didn't record this last visit in the dark-room?" Anderson asked.

"No, I wasn't expecting him there. I think that they can track people now so I should keep a camera handy at all times." Patrick made a mental note.

"I would like to see this place of yours, the scene of the crime so to speak," Anderson said, "Would next Saturday be convenient?"

"Does this mean that you believe us?" Mary was wide-eyed with surprise.

Anderson looked at her earnestly, "It means that I don't disbelieve you! Something unusual has happened, of that I'm sure and now all we have to do is decide what it was."

CHAPTER TWENTY-SIX

"So this is where it all started!" Anderson looked around the apartment, noticing the camera and its blinking red light.

"I was sitting on the sofa when the finger appeared," Mary explained, "but I was in the kitchen when I first noticed the lights. The heads appeared later in that corner." She flung her hand at the far corner.

"And they always appeared at the same point?" Anderson looked at the corner thoughtfully.

Mary nodded, "The lights would appear anywhere but at first they were in the same place."

"You said that you had some recordings, is it possible to see them now?" Anderson turned to Patrick.

Patrick produced a flash-drive and plugged it into the laptop. He showed Anderson the various manifestations of lights and heads and the astronomer listened very carefully to the conversations without saying a word. The recordings of atmospheric changes he only glanced at but his eyes didn't miss a thing.

When the presentation was finished, Anderson sat quietly thinking; the others waited expectantly for his verdict.

Finally, he raised his head, "The trouble with these recordings is that today it is easy to fake something!" He held his hand up to forestall their objections, "I'm not saying that they are fake, simply that some people, most people would say that. We need irrefutable proof!"

"What sort of proof?" Patrick asked.

Anderson shrugged, "Perhaps if I can talk to this Charlie I can arrange something but you say that his appearances are random. I can't stay here until he appears again! It's a pity that you don't have a recording of the last time; it sounded very interesting!"

"Do you believe us?" Mary asked nervously.

"It is still the same answer, I don't disbelieve and certainly something has happened. The problem is in deciding what!" Clive shrugged his shoulders.

"What shall we do now?" Patrick asked.

"Can you give me a copy of those recordings? I would advise you to continue recording. If possible you could carry a camera on you at all times, both of you, so that you don't miss anything."

"I can use my mobile," Mary suggested, "I don't feel happy in carrying around a camera, however small it is!"

"I don't have any problem with that, after all, I'm used to doing just that!" Patrick confirmed.

Anderson waved a finger, "When this Charlie appears next time, tell him that I would like to meet him. You can tell him who I am and what I am attempting to do. If he is a prankster, he will not agree or not show up and that would remove one doubt."

"He may have a difficulty in stating a precise time; it's been so haphazard so far!" Patrick said.

"Ask all the same! I can make myself free on a particular day if that is possible." Anderson reached down and pick up a book from the coffee table, "Is this what you have been reading?" He looked at the other books, pulled out a pen and notebook and starting writing. "These are some that I recommend."

Mary took the note, "Thank you, we've been trying to find the right ones. A bit hopeless when you don't know what the subject is!"

"The authors are the main point; they are experts and you can read anything that they have written." Anderson said.

He stayed for a while longer, probably hoping that Charlie would appear but he didn't and the astronomer left.

"What do you think?" Mary asked as they walked back into the living room.

"I think that he's genuinely interested even if it is a fake. He didn't come right out and dismiss it." Patrick looked happy.

"Do you think that it could be fake?" Mary sat down in the armchair and crossed her legs.

"It could be!" Patrick sat on the sofa, "I don't see how it can be done but I think that it's the real McCoy. What really convinces me is that notice on the bus; that couldn't be faked!"

Mary leaned back and closed her eyes, "Every time we deal with this problem, even if Charlie isn't here, I feel exhausted."

"If you're up to it, I'll take you for a pub lunch." Patrick offered.

"I hope that includes a few drinks – for medicinal purposes!"

CHAPTER TWENTY-SEVEN

On the Sunday, they had a surprise; Mary's friends arrived unannounced! Their curiosity had got the better of them and so five young ladies arrived at the door just before lunch.

Mary glared at them when she opened the door; she knew full well that they had come to inspect the boyfriend! They ignored her glare and entered, giggling like schoolgirls.

"We bought some cake and some cheap plonk, so get some plates and glasses out!" said one, waving a bottle of supermarket wine.

Patrick stood and waited for the initial inspection, a polite smile on his face. Soon would come the interrogation; where are you from? Do you have any brothers and sisters? What car do you drive? And where do you work?

Patrick had to fetch the dining chairs in for everyone to have a seat. They were full of gossip, the main offender was a red-head called Gwen, chattering non-stop as her eyes travelled around the room to see what changes the boyfriend had created.

Mary started to pick up the books from the coffee table and another girl called Alice took one, "My God! You are into heavy reading! Is there a section on horoscopes?"

Patrick produced a tight smile, "This is about astronomy; astrology is something completely different!"

Alice ignored his words and his outstretched hand and placed the book back on the table and continued talking, "Did you see my horoscope yesterday? Libra, it said that the day would be full of woe and it was! I laddered my tights, the heel broke on my shoe, and the deli had run out of that delicate sauce. What is the world coming to?"

"What indeed!" Patrick muttered and wished Charlie would put on one of his displays!

"Don't talk to me about horoscopes!" Gwen said in a loud voice, "My sister ignored the warnings the other day, and…."

A switch clicked off in Patrick's head, cutting out the voices and inane chatter. He took a sip of wine and noticed a brunette sitting at the other end of the sofa to Gwen. There was a faint smile on her face and she was staring off into space, somehow detached from the nonsense around her. She caught Patrick's stare and her eyebrows lifted. Silently her lips formed the word, 'sorry'.

Patrick smiled his thanks! At least one of them seemed to be more down-to-earth!

"Patrick! Or is it Pat?" Gwen called out. The switch in his head snapped back on.

"Oh, eh, I prefer Patrick. What were you saying?"

"Mary was saying that you work at the polytechnic. Does that make you a teacher?" He was asked.

Patrick smiled politely, "Hardly! I instruct on photographic technique. I wouldn't really call it teaching!"

Gwen turned her head away, effectively dismissing Patrick as uninteresting. "My nephew took some stunning photographs while on holiday at Easter, and…." The switch in Patrick's head snapped off again.

He sat politely mute, sipping wine and looking patient. He offered to make coffee and escaped into the kitchen. He ran his hands over his face and hair and heard someone behind him. He turned and saw that it was the apologetic brunette.

"I thought to come and help you and to introduce myself, I'm Jeanette!" She held her hand out and Patrick shook it. "I shouldn't mind Gwen, she has her good points but now you're seeing her at her worst!"

"I wouldn't have guessed!" Patrick smiled, "How do they like their coffee?"

"All with milk and no sugar, except me, I'll take it black with sugar."

"You seem out of place with the others," Patrick ventured.

"They're all office workers, probably why they gossip, but I work in a laboratory. We tend to keep our heads over the microscope and say little."

"Ah, would you be so kind as to take in the tray with their coffee and I'll bring yours and ours." Patrick searched for a smaller tray.

Patrick had never observed anyone talking, eating, and drinking all at the same time before, but Gwen managed very well!

Eventually the cake was eaten and the bottles were empty, so they left. Dutifully, Patrick bade each of them goodbye and hoped they would come again. His left hand was behind his back with his fingers crossed!

"Phew! I am so sorry for that!" Mary collapsed in the armchair.

"Don't apologise! In a way they were amusing but it was a good job that Charlie didn't appear; I think that would have kept them quiet!"

"Oh my God, I never thought of that!" Mary held a hand up to her face.

"For a while I was hoping that he would!" Patrick chuckled.

"Gwen was showing off! She does that every time she meets a new man, especially someone else's!" her mouth twisted to show her disapproval.

Patrick started to clear the debris from the table but Mary jumped up, "I'll help with that, then we'll have a pot of tea and try to recover our senses!"

CHAPTER TWENTY-EIGHT

Clive Anderson had arrived back home, his mind in a brown study over the meeting with Mary and Patrick. He would have to bone up on the extreme ideas of some of his colleagues; he didn't usually pay very much attention to them, they were more suited to science fiction!

He felt uneasy for some unknown reason, or perhaps it was excitement. The recordings of the image were very convincing and if it was a prank, it was a very good one! He didn't think that the couple were behind it, just victims or perhaps witnesses.

After greeting his family and saying a few words, he retired into his study. He sat just thinking of what he did know about extreme theories and what he had learned about this 'Charlie'. Why Charlie for God's sake? Surely he could have picked a better name!

He/they were long-lived, if not immortal. Patrick said that they had been around since the Big Bang which meant fourteen or so billion years! What sort of life form could live so long? It suggested that there was no form of sexual reproduction and a lack of entropy; surely everything wears out!

Then there is the problem that their matter and energy is different to ours, not compatible. Are they made of anti-matter? Could the Big Bang have produced two separate systems of energy and matter? Could there be more universes with even more different systems?

They had a type of distance, (what does that mean?) but they have no need to travel. Clive sat back in his chair and tried to imagine such a universe. Very slowly he began to stitch together some shaky theories of what happened there in Charlie's universe. None of them he would voice in public or even leave a few notes; he would lose all credibility with mainstream cosmologists and astronomers.

There was a gentle knock on the door and his wife's head appeared through the open door. "Are you alright? You looked very pale and worried when you came home."

Clive smiled encouragingly, "No sweetheart, nothing of importance, just a technical headache!"

"Oh good! I was so worried! Dinner soon; would you fetch the children in?"

As Clive stood and walked into the garden, he thought that if Charlie were for real there would be some serious repercussions! First of all, is this true or false? Is someone playing a hoax? Assuming that this is real, what he had heard revealed a world that was nothing like this one!

The laws of physics, most of them, do not apply on Charlie's world and that makes it hard to visualise; even basic things like up and down may not apply!

He was lost in thought, standing in the centre of the lawn while the children continued to play. After a while, Rachel came to the French windows.

"Clive! Please bring the children in!"

"What? Oh yes, sorry about that, lost in thought. C'mon kids, wash your hands and we'll see what sort of feast we shall have!" He managed to maintain his usual banter with the children and his wife through the meal and even while helping with the washing up but after that he slipped by degrees into deeper thought. Rachel was quite accustomed to this and she wasn't surprised when his thoughts guided his feet back to his study.

He selected two books from the shelves and sat down to read. String theory was really cosmology, where physics and astronomy shared a common bond and he had never taken an especially keen interest in M-theory. The simple reason was that if membranes did exist, there was no way that an astronomer could observe them.

He decided to call a colleague, a physicist at the research centre at Brookhaven, but when he rang all he got was a recorded message. Then he remembered that his friend was at a conference, so he called another.

"Phil, how are you? I hope that I'm not intruding!" He used the loudspeaker.

"Not really!" Phil answered, "I know that you astronomers don't sleep at night! What can I do for you?"

This was a problem! He did not want to reveal the true reason that he was calling, partly because he felt embarrassed at dealing with something that could be a hoax. Reputations could be lost!

"I've been thinking about the Big Bang and what really happened then." He tried to make it a casual approach.

"You obviously don't have too much work on! You do realise that the Big Bang is just a theory and will probably remain so, however, what is actually on your mind?"

Clive took the plunge! "In a word, membranes! There are suggestions that when the event occurred, several membranes were created and they would lead to different types of particles and energies."

"Actually there is a suggestion that membranes have always existed and that two touched and created our universe." Clive could imagine that Phil was settling back in his chair and preparing for a long discussion.

"If that is the case, surely there could be more than one universe created?" Clive suggested.

Phil chuckled, "You are mixing up your theories! Big Bang, membranes and multi-verse, you're just making a headache for yourself! It is possible that there is something of each in the creation theory. Where are you heading with this? You wouldn't be thinking of Dark Matter would you?"

Clive silently thanked Phil for providing a plausible excuse for Clive's questions and late 'phone call. "Frankly, I

THE Dancing Lights

don't know where I'm heading but if there is at least another universe on another membrane, one that we cannot detect, what sort of physics would it have?"

"Phew! Let me think about that!" Phil went silent for a few minutes, "I'm not so sure that we cannot detect the other universe! There is the question of why gravity is so weak and it has been suggested that we could be sharing gravity with another universe. Even if we accept Dark Matter and Dark Energy, they could also be shared with another universe. We can only detect them because of the effect that they make in our universe."

"I've got that already," Clive answered, "But I was thinking about the particles. If they had electrons, neutrons, and protons, we would be able to see them and the same would apply to photons. I was wondering how their matter could be made up without using our type of particles."

"I assume that you have dismissed anti-matter, because we can detect that!" Phil went quiet and Clive asked if he was still there, "Yeah, yeah, let me think a while!" and he fell silent again.

Clive fetched another book from the shelves and opened it. He became absorbed in the text and time passed and his call forgotten, so he started with surprise when Phil started to talk.

"We cannot assume anything," the physicist said, "Quarks make up the protons and neutrons, hanging together with the aid of gluons. The strong and weak energies make everything work with the electrons and making up the different elements. Even a slight deviation in their values would negate matter and prevent it forming. If matter exists undetected in this other universe then all of the energies would be entirely different to ours. Remember that matter is only a form of energy. We are talking about something beyond our wildest imagination and mathematics, a totally new regime of energies!"

"Is there any way that you can describe those energies?" Clive asked.

"Not a hope! How serious is your question? I'm asking because you have roused my interest; what sort of energies could be possible to form matter but we could not see, touch, or smell? Not just the opposite like anti-matter, something at the other end of a different spectrum! Because of that, space and time would be anti-Einstein, utterly impossible!"

"That fits in with my thoughts," Clive said thoughtfully, "It is a serious question and I like your term, 'anti-Einstein', it would make nonsense of his relativity!"

"You can say that again! I can run it through some guys over here, I have a few bright students who are looking for something to do. Leave it with me but I'm not certain when I'll get back to you."

Clive thanked him and closed the line. Phil had confirmed what he had thought and he smiled. 'Anti-Einstein' was a perfect description, even if it lacked any details!

CHAPTER TWENTY-NINE

Charlie arrived just as Mary returned home from work. Patrick was in the kitchen making some tea for her arrival and was not aware that Charlie had put on an appearance until Mary called out.

Carrying the tray of cups and teapot, he entered the living room to see the now familiar grey face of Charlie hovering in the corner. Mary was transfixed in the doorway, her face showing the apprehension that she felt.

"Hi Charlie, how are you today?" Patrick made it sound as normal as possible that aliens popped in for tea every afternoon! It was for Mary's benefit, before she started screaming or crying.

"Thank you Patrick, it is good to contact you again and you too Mary." If anything the face appeared to be more realistic, although devoid of any other colour than grey. His cycs turned towards Mary when he addressed her and that was something new.

"We have a friend who wants to meet you but we have to fix a date. Is that possible?" Patrick asked.

As usual when asked a question, Charlie's face froze for a moment and then he replied. "It is most difficult to arrange for a precise time but I can say that I'll be here in three days' time. Is that accurate enough?"

"We will tell him but I think that it will be alright." Patrick poured out the tea.

"What is that you are doing?" Charlie's eyes were following every move.

"This is called tea. A few times every day, the majority of us drink this or something similar as a way to relax." Patrick looked at the grey head, "Don't you do something like this?"

"We have no need," Charlie answered, "Can you exist without it?"

"We do need to drink water frequently, this just gives it a pleasant flavour." Patrick held the cup up for Charlie to see.

"This is the first time I have been able to have a conversation with your people," the grey head said, "Things like this tea I wondered about; I had seen this many times and questioned its significance. Who is this friend that wishes to talk to me?"

Patrick sat down next to Mary on the sofa, mainly to give her some comfort as she still looked tense. "His name is Clive and he is one of our scientists. I'm sure that he will have many questions for you!"

"And I for him!" Charlie agreed.

"I have a question of my own," Patrick settled back in the sofa, "You said earlier that you have visited us many times and yet now you say that this is the first time you have had a conversation. I find that peculiar!"

Charlie's face froze for a moment and then became animated once more. "It is very difficult for me to create this image and that was only achieved after a long period of trying to project into your world. At first I could only observe but now I have managed to control the sound."

"Every time we ask a question your face stops moving," Patrick said, "and you always say 'I', but I'm sure that there is more than one of you. Is that correct?"

Charlie's face broke into a rare smile, "I thought that you were intelligent! Yes, the face freezes because I am in conference but we have a different concept of personalities, the 'I' and 'we' that you have."

Mary shuddered, "I find that this is confusing and that terrifies me! What are you?"

Charlie's face froze for a longer time but eventually it turned to Mary. "I do not mean to alarm you! You have no reason to be afraid! It is difficult for me to answer your question but I will try. On your world you have many creatures, most of which do not look like you or behave like you but all of those creatures have a common source, a common ancestor. I, we are simply another form of life but as different from all your life forms as you are from an amoeba."

"But you know our language very well and none of our creatures can do that!" Mary's voice quivered on the verge of breaking.

"As I have said, we have observed you for a long period and during that time we have learned your language and many of the others on your world. We have just one language!"

"Do – do you have a religion?" Mary was surprised at her own question, considering that she had no really strong religion.

Charlie didn't freeze at this question, "Religion is a belief and very important to intelligent creatures. You have many religions but we have just one belief and it involves the nature of our world and is difficult to describe because of that. In short, we do have a religion but not as you would recognise!"

"You believe in God?" Mary asked again.

"We believe in the nature of one!" came the enigmatic reply.

"I think that we have had a good chat Charlie, can you leave us until Clive is with us?" Patrick requested.

"Of course, I can see that Mary is troubled but there is no need to be! Until three days' time." The grey face faded quietly from view.

"Why did you ask about religion?" Patrick turned to her when the visage finally disappeared.

Mary shrugged, "Perhaps it would make him appear more human!"

"Did it? Charlie doesn't live in a world like this one, so I don't think that anything that we have has any relevance to him or them!"

"He believes in something beyond the here and now and that must give him a sense of morals, of justice or whatever! I think that his answer satisfies me that he is something to trust. How much that trust goes is another question!" Mary explained.

Patrick thought for a while, sipping his tea in quiet contemplation. "I see what you mean but it all depends on what he thinks is moral and justice. We don't give much thought to the lower life forms and he might consider us to be living in a puddle!"

CHAPTER THIRTY

Clive arrived at 6am, catching the pair at an early breakfast. All he carried was an attaché case, from which he took a small recorder and placing it on the table he accepted a cup of coffee.

"I have been asking some colleagues of mine about what sort of things would exist in another universe," he informed them.

"And what did they tell you?" Mary asked.

"Not a lot!" Clive said wryly, "Some came up with some mathematical formulae but we couldn't understand what they indicated. Yes, it is possible that other types of physics to exist but translating that into normal terms was hopeless!"

"What did you think about our last conversation with Charlie?" Patrick was eager to find out what the astronomer thought.

"Very interesting! It matches some of the ideas that we have, although it is still difficult to picture. What we have to remember that his reality is totally different to ours and I'm surprised that he managed to make contact at all!"

"What did you think about his religion?" Mary asked.

"He didn't say anything!" Clive gestured, "Every creature has to believe in something, even if it is just that there will be a tomorrow. Some of our ancestors believed that the sun rose because they prayed to their god. What I found intriguing was that he said that he believed in one! I can interpret that in several ways!"

"What I can't get my head round is that he is an alien!" Mary clutched her shoulders as though she was cold. "I could believe ET landing in a space ship but this is totally weird!"

"I wonder which of them would be the more worrisome. At least Charlie isn't here physically!" Clive pointed out.

Mary gave another shudder, "That thought really makes me very frightened!"

"He seems to be an amiable character!" Patrick pointed out.

"Thank you Patrick!" The voice appeared before the image of the grey face which gradually came into focus. "I really mean you no harm; I'm just curious!"

"Hello Charlie, we have our friend Clive with us." Patrick turned towards the grey face.

"Hello Clive, very pleased to meet you. How can I be of service?" Charlie sounded very convivial.

"Hello Charlie, pleased to meet you too!" Clive had been surprised by the voice and the face but now switched on his recorder and studied the image. "Why the name Charlie?"

A smile appeared on the face, "I found out that it has comical associations. It was simple and innocuous and that projected a friendly person, which I am!"

"You say 'I', and yet you have indicated that there are more than just one of you. Can you please explain?" Clive leaned forward, whether to get a better view or to listen better wasn't clear.

The answer surprised them! "We are not detached like you! We are individuals but not completely isolated, prisoners of our own thoughts and fears. Whatever one of us thinks or does is known by the others."

"Is that why you don't have to travel?" Patrick interrupted, "If you want to see or know something, one of the others does so and you all know."

"Something like that!" Charlie still did not give firm replies.

Clive continued his questions, "How many of you are there?"

"The simple answer is one!" Charlie said softly, "We are not individuals, separate entities as you are. Each of us is part of another and the essence of each and every one of us is carried by all."

"Do you occupy all of your world or only a part of it?" Clive asked.

"We occupy our entire universe! There is not a part of our universe that we do not know! We have no need of cars, rockets, or bicycles to find anything new as you are doing!"

"There must be billions of you!" Mary gasped.

"If we were humans, the number would be billions of trillions but we are only one!" Charlie continued to use that calm, soft voice as though explaining to children.

The thought prompted another question from Clive, "Are there any children?"

"When you reproduce, two entities, a man and a woman couple to produce a third entity, the child, which is in essence a blend of the first two entities," Charlie explained, "We are only one entity, our parts are already blended and we have no need for children!"

Mary and Patrick's mouths fell open. "Do you not love and cherish each other?" Mary asked, a touch of pity entering her voice.

"I love myself, don't you?" Charlie said.

"Sometimes I don't!" Mary answered, "I can be beastly to some people!"

"But we cannot do that to ourselves!" Charlie's soft voice was almost hypnotic. "Our thoughts and fears are known and therefore there can be no fear or adverse thoughts!"

"You make it sound as though you have no emotions!" Mary continued.

"We do not have grand passions as you but we can and do care for our various parts!" Charlie answered.

"There is such a thing called entropy," Clive took control of the conversation again, although he had a feeling that he wasn't, "Everything needs energy and this dissipates over time, things die."

"We know of this entropy, we have observed things dying in your world but it is only a part of something that you call evolution." Charlie's voice made Patrick's eyes partly close. He shook himself awake to continue listening. "Nothing really dies! A sun loses its energy and in doing so it casts its substance into the void, creating material for new suns. It is the same with everything!"

"Your suns do not explode?" Clive frowned at the answers he was given. The next answer shocked him!

"We do not have suns or planets!"

"Then what are you standing on?" Patrick burst out.

"What is standing? It is the resistance of matter against matter, under the influence of gravity!" Charlie answered his own question.

"Do you have atoms and particles?" Clive asked.

"If you refer to your own science, you will know that all matter is a form of energy," Charlie's face appeared to smile, "We do have particles but they do not react as yours do. When the old universe divided, the energies went to different places. Some of them evolved into what you observe around you and others came here and other places. Some energy could not survive and vanished by turning into something else; your world came into being. The same happened here but a different world was created. Some energy is shared between the worlds."

"We have something we call Dark Energy. It's a complete mystery," Clive said, "Is that something we share with you? It causes the universe to expand."

Charlie's face froze for quite a long period and then the grey head shook from side to side, "We have no such thing here but it may be from another universe."

"A third one!" Patrick exclaimed, "How many are there?"

"We have no idea!" Charlie said, "When what you call the Big Bang occurred, many universes were created, at least that is our feeling."

"How do you project this image?" Clive asked.

"We do not project an image! Anything we make here cannot exist in your world. You have no name or theory for the type of world we live in but we can manipulate things like photons. It took a long time to be able to control photons to create this image and even longer to create sound and place the image with any accuracy." Charlie turned his head towards Mary, "I apologise for some of the things we created but they were in the nature of experiments and we had little control at that time."

"Just a moment!" Patrick frowned, "This all started a couple of months ago but you say that it took a long time!"

"Our time passes at a different rate than yours and our worlds do not coincide in time and place every time. That has been our major difficulty – arriving in your world in a linear sequence and at the same place."

"I'm still puzzled over this machine you use to communicate," Clive leaned even nearer towards the grey head.

"You mean a device that performs a function?" Charlie smiled again, "It is not a machine in your sense of the word. There are no knobs and dials – it just is! I think one of the problems that we are going to have is in describing each other's worlds!"

"That is obvious!" Clive grunted, "Could you leave us for a while? We need to think about what you have said."

"Certainly! Enjoy your tea!" Charlie faded from sight.

"What do you think of him?" Patrick asked Clive after the image faded.

Clive wiped his face and shook his head, "I don't know where to begin! It is not really my field but what he says does tie in with the little I know." He turned off the recorder and stared at it.

"I don't know anything about the science but I don't know if to feel sorry for him – I mean them!" Mary had lost that look of nervousness and looked thoughtfully at her hands, "Imagine a world without passion! The great music and art or just a good belly laugh!"

"A world without our extremes!" Patrick murmured, "It sounds a bit boring!"

"I sometimes think that this world is too exciting!" Clive stood and walked up and down, "I'm going to have to talk to my colleague again and he is going to think I'm losing it!"

CHAPTER THIRTY-ONE

"Phil, please don't hang up! I have been talking to an ET and I need someone to talk to," Clive crossed his fingers and hoped!

"I think that this is where I agree with you and I can suggest a doctor!" Phil replied with humour.

"I knew that you would take that stance!" Clive sighed. This was going to be the main problem – convincing people he wasn't delusional! "Just hear me out and then you can make a decision."

"Is this something to do with what other worlds would be like?" Phil asked.

"Yes it is but I'll start at the beginning." Clive related the story, starting with Mary's experience and up to his conversation with Charlie. He left out Mary and Patrick's names for their protection.

"And you say that this creature calls itself Charlie?" Phil asked when Clive had finished.

"I know, I had the same reaction!" Clive answered, "If it had been Spiff it would have sounded better."

"I'm not so sure! It sounds stupid enough to be true!" Phil sounded thoughtful.

"So what do you think of what he said?" Clive waited for the reply but there was just a long silence. "Are you still there?"

"Yeah, I'm still here and I'm wondering why! It sounds crazy enough to be true! There has been speculation about other life forms but this is way past any of that, at least the sensible suggestions! Can you send me an account of what has happened and don't use the Internet, it leaks like a sieve! Use the post."

"I can send the recording I made as well and there are some video recordings that the fellow made. I can put it all on a CD. Does this mean that you're going to take this seriously?" Clive asked.

Phil sighed, "Up to a point! If it were anyone else than you, I'd be ringing the funny farm! I'll go as far as exploring the physics that this Charlie claims his world has but I'm not buying into the ET thing, at least not yet!"

"Thanks Phil! I know that this will go somewhere!" Clive stated firmly.

"As long as it isn't some prank by someone! Remember that Feynman was a great practical joker!" Phil reminded him.

"I don't think that it is anyone like that!" Clive smiled as he recalled Feynman's many pranks, "If it was a physicist they wouldn't target an unknown couple, it would have been you and me!"

"But we've been hooked anyway!" Phil pointed out.

CHAPTER THIRTY-TWO

Clive made the journey to the apartment early the following Saturday, as he wanted to catch them off-guard. Phil's apprehension that this was a hoax was contagious!

Mary and Patrick were simply surprised to see him at the door; there was no sign of guilt or nervousness, in fact they appeared pleased to see him.

He had an excuse ready, "I apologise for intruding unannounced but I lost your 'phone number."

"No problem!" Patrick said, "Come in, we're just having breakfast."

"I have been speaking to one of my colleagues," Clive explained, "He would like copies of your videos and the data that you recorded. Can we get them on a CD?"

"I already made copies, so there's no problem at all! Instant service!" Patrick produced two CDs.

"Did the…did Charlie make another appearance?" Clive asked as he accepted a large mug of coffee.

"Yeah, he came back just after you left," Patrick answered, "Not much to tell and it's on the CD."

"I asked him about how he lived," Mary's hair looked tousled. Obviously she had not had time to brush it. "I still feel a bit sorry for him – or them. There doesn't seem to be any joy in their lives!"

"Perhaps they get joy and satisfaction in ways that we cannot comprehend," Clive offered.

"But a life devoid of colour, of great works of music, or Rembrandt, or the glory of a fine sunset," Mary frowned, "How can they call that living?"

"If you had never seen a sunset, or heard Mozart, would you miss them? Would you ever understand them?" Clive countered.

"But now we have introduced those concepts," Mary answered back, "Now they know that beauty can exist. Won't that have some effect?"

"I havè no idea!" Clive shrugged, "They may be wired differently and couldn't appreciate them, or perhaps they will now seek out those things in their world."

Mary shook her head, "I asked him and he said that he didn't understand why we had dark and light times; they don't have days and nights!"

"There are planets in our universe that have two or more suns and therefore they never experience night!" Clive informed her.

"They never see the stars? How awful! How unromantic!" Mary looked cross.

"They don't have children so there is no need to be romantic!" Patrick pointed out, "It does seem to be a boring place and they've been like that for billions of years!"

"Blind people can appreciate the description of a fine painting or a sunset!" Mary pouted her lips, "Beethoven produced his greatest works when he was deaf! Charlie is worse than blind or deaf!"

"None-the-less, he or they are like that, as we are like we are and we just have to accept that!" Clive advised her.

"But how will they understand us if we say we're going to look at the night sky?" Mary wailed.

"With any luck they will probably think that we are a little eccentric!" Clive smiled at the thought.

"Not really Clive!" They were startled by Charlie's voice and gradually his face appeared. "We realise that there are profound differences in our two peoples but that does not have to exclude understanding!"

"Were you eavesdropping on us?" Patrick asked with more than a little indignation.

"Not intentionally!" the grey face answered, "I had just tuned in and heard your remarks and delayed appearing so that you could finish your conversation. The mere fact that I admit to overhearing you proves that there was no ill intent."

"I am still trying to understand your lives," Clive changed topic, "There does not appear to be very much substance in your world! You don't sit or stand, walk or run and you don't have worlds that rotate. That seems very odd to us!"

"I wish that you could experience my world," Charlie said a little wistfully, "We lack nothing and we are satisfied with what we can see, even if we do not have a Rembrandt or a Beethoven."

"How do you see our world?" Clive asked.

"Not as you do!" Charlie said, "We sense your presence and that is how we first discovered that there was another world. You were just there!"

"But you call us by name," Clive looked very interested, "Can you actually sense a difference between us?"

"Oh yes! It is very clear to me which of you is Clive, Mary, and Patrick, as clear to us as the other creatures in your universe."

Tight lines appeared around Clive's mouth and his eyes widened, "Do you mean universe or world?"

"I mean universe with the same meaning as yours." Charlie clarified, "We do know that there are many worlds in your universe and on many there are other creatures."

The scene froze, even the dust motes appeared not to move. No one uttered a sound. Mary covered her open mouth with her hand and Patrick stared at the grey face with an amazed expression. Clive felt as though his head was about to burst open. Everyone understood the implication in Charlie's words!

Clive made two attempts to break the silence, "Do you…can you talk to these other creatures?"

"Some of them!" Charlie answered, "Many of them are weak, or do I mean poor? We try but there is no intelligence there, while others have very strong intelligence."

"Where are these creatures?" Clive croaked.

"On other worlds, I thought that I told you that! If you want to know where, I'm afraid that I can't help you as we do not understand your spatial references!"

Clive really did feel as though his head had burst! Here was a creature that could prove that there was other life in the universe but he could not supply directions! He flopped back in the armchair with a gasp, his mouth wide open.

"Are you alright?" Mary asked in a worried voice.

Silently Clive nodded and then covered his face with both hands. He felt like shouting, screaming at the grey face, at the stupidity, the comedy of the situation!

"I seem to have upset you! That was not my intention!" Charlie actually sounded worried.

Clive nodded, "It's not your fault Charlie and it's just that we have been trying to contact these other creatures but we were not sure that they existed or where they were. You could have supplied all of the answers to our questions!"

"Perhaps he still can, if we get enough clues!" Mary said.

Clive shook his head, "Charlie, how big are we? How big is our world?"

"I cannot answer that in a way that is intelligible! We have no concept of measurement!" Charlie said.

Clive turned to Mary, "That's the problem, he can't supply distance or direction, only 'thataway' but it may as well be 'whichaway'! He can't even tell us what sort of creatures they are!"

"I do apologise!" Charlie didn't sound apologetic, "There is not much I can do to help but I could tell you all I do know of these creatures."

Clive waved a hand, "Don't trouble yourself, we can record all that you do know and that will help a lot but we'll have to think out this problem so that you can give directions."

"I can withdraw now and perhaps we can find a solution." Charlie offered.

"Thank you Charlie! At least it's a small step in the right direction!" Clive sounded utterly dejected.

The grey face disappeared and everyone sat quietly, Clive leaning back in the armchair with his eyes closed. "This could have been the shining achievement to my career!" Clive said in a thoughtful tone.

"It still can!" Patrick came alive, "We'll have to use what we have and make the best of that!"

"Making a pig's ear out of a silk purse!" Clive smiled at his own jest.

"No, Patrick's right!" Mary exclaimed, "If we collect the data that Charlie has now, it will serve a purpose in the future but we can also teach Charlie about our measurement systems. Then we will know where to aim our telescopes and those large dishes."

Clive's eyes blinked open, "We can try but do you realise that Charlie will be trying to find places as though he was blindfolded in a dark room and then reaching through a letterbox into the outside and unknown world. It's going to be difficult!"

"But you're not giving up!" Mary smiled encouragingly, "I have some whiskey somewhere and I think that this deserves a toast!"

CHAPTER THIRTY-THREE

"What happens now?" Mary asked.

"What do you mean?" She and Patrick were walking in the park.

"Well, Charlie is going to tell us everything he knows and most of it will only make sense to Clive. We seem to be dropping out of the picture!"

"I'm not so sure that's going to happen!" Patrick kicked a ball back to a group of children, "From what we've heard the major problem is creating a system that both sides can understand and until that is done there will not be any progress!"

"Are you suggesting that we're at a dead end?" Mary tugged at his arm.

Patrick stopped walking, threw back his head and studied the trees. He contemplated the question, trying to find a suitable answer. "I hate to say that we are but Charlie's world has no idea of direction or of distance and everything is made up of some very strange substances. It's a big challenge to both Charlie and Clive!"

"I can't even start to imagine Charlie's world!" Mary slipped her arm into his, making him resume walking. "When I was a kid I loved Alice in Wonderland and I'm trying to think like Lewis Carroll; how would he describe it to Alice?"

"We have all of the characters in one! Charlie is the Cheshire Cat, the Caterpillar, Humpty Dumpty and the Mad Hatter. Trying to make sense out of those would give anyone a headache!" Patrick gave a small laugh.

"I'm glad that you said the Cheshire Cat, because that is what Charlie appears to be; he pops in and out of view and in bits just like the cat!" Mary said.

Patrick stopped again and stared at Mary, "It's funny that you brought up Alice in Wonderland. I had an uncle who loved the Goon Show; it was a comedy that starred Peter

Sellers, Spike Milligan, Michael Bentine, and Harry Secombe, and a few others. It was absolute madness! It centred on all things that were most unlikely, improbable, and absolutely impossible. I remember in one sketch, that they hid a battleship in a desert oasis – by floating it on end!"

"What's the connection to Alice in Wonderland?"

"Well, I never read Alice in Wonderland, but Milligan, Sellers, and a few others performed in a film version and that I did see. I think that they were perfect for the parts and they could have easily used the name Charlie in one of their sketches like this!"

Mary smiled, "Are you telling me that this is really a comedy?"

"It certainly is as bizarre as one of the Goon sketches!" Patrick smiled back and he continued walking, his free hand holding her arm folded in his, "or Alice's adventures!"

"So you don't believe in Charlie?" Mary looked up in to his face.

"No! I believe that Charlie is everything he claims to be! I just can't see Clive making any sense out of this!" Patrick gestured with his free hand.

There was a display by some youngsters on roller-blades, part mime and part dance. Mary pulled Patrick over to watch and they shelved their discussion. Patrick was glad for that, his mind was bubbling over with images of Spike Milligan playing the part of Charlie.

The show stopped and one of the players came round with a hat. Mary and Patrick gave a few coins.

"I think that from our point of view we should sit back and have a laugh at the antics of Clive and Charlie!" Patrick said as they resumed walking. "If we take it too seriously we could go mad!"

"Perhaps Charlie would transfer his appearance over to where Clive works," Mary said thoughtfully, "That would not disturb us. I'll buy you an ice-cream!" She changed the subject as they came to an ice-cream van.

Taking their ice-cream cornets over to the grass, they sat down under a maple tree.

"If Charlie moves over to Clive; that leaves us with nothing to do!" She watched Patrick chase a melting piece of ice cream before it ran over his fingers.

"Maybe, maybe not!" Patrick took a huge bite of ice cream. "It may be easier for Charlie to focus on us and perhaps he is studying us, which he couldn't do as well if he was stuck in Clive's office or laboratory."

"Do you really think that he is studying us?" Mary nibbled her ice cream delicately.

"If you could see him in his world, wouldn't you be just a little curious?" Patrick wiped his mouth on his handkerchief, "I don't think that he sees us as we would see things. I get the impression that he senses us in other ways."

"What other ways?"

"Ah! There you have the crux of the problem! How does a blind man see?"

CHAPTER THIRTY-FOUR

Clive was asking himself the same question! He was staring at his notepad, where he had jotted down the few facts that he knew about Charlie's universe.

According to him:

· He was the only creature in that universe,

· But he was a creature of many parts,

· He did not have to travel anywhere, as he was already there.

· Because of this, he had no perception of north, south, east, west, up, or down.

· if he didn't travel, he did not understand the concept of distance or speed.

· That implied that time was something strange to him, although possibly he did live in a world with sequential time.

· How did he understand our universe? If he had no concept of distance, the basic 3-dimensions, how could he make the face?

His wife had gone to bed long ago. He had promised faithfully that he wouldn't be long, but now it was after 3 am! He sighed and rubbed his face. It was too late to ring Phil, even he went to bed at normal times!

Clive wondered how Charlie understood this universe. He had made a 3-dimensional face but was that just mimicking what he perceived. Probably, and he remembered that the first face was a copy of Mary's face.

Then there were the early faces that showed the inner parts of the skull. Whatever they had as vision could see into a solid body, like an X-ray.

Clive scribbled a few questions for the next time he spoke to Charlie, and then decided that he should at least get a few hours sleep.

He awoke in the morning at the sound of the children playing in the garden and the smell of coffee and bacon. With a grunt he sat up and shook his head. It was full of cobwebs and he made his way blearily to the shower.

Feeling as though he could at least face part of the day, he greeted his wife and poured a large mug of coffee. He needed that! Fortified by the coffee and breakfast he went into the garden and filled his lungs with fresh air.

Rachel appeared at his side with another coffee, "What time did you get to bed last night?" she asked.

"Very late! Early morning in fact!" Clive accepted the coffee.

"I think that you left something switched on. There was something buzzing in the study but I couldn't see anything," she said.

Clive frowned. There wasn't anything in the study that buzzed! Perhaps it was an electrical short in something; he'd check it out in a while.

"What are you working on now?" Rachel took a keen and supportive interest in her husband's work.

"Something really weird!" Clive wondered briefly if he should tell her this early in the investigation about Charlie, it could still be a hoax but he decided to go ahead.

"What would you say if I told you that I had been speaking to an alien?" He kept a straight face and continued staring over the lawn.

"I would think that you've been into the sherry too much!" Rachel looked up at his face and saw that it wasn't a joke.

"It's a strange story," he said, "A young couple came to me asking about life in other universes. It was immediately apparent that something had happened to raise the question in their minds. Usually I get questions about little green men but this was different. I went to their apartment and this face appeared and spoke to us." He looked down at her and saw that she was considering all possible reasons.

"Just a face?" Rachel pulled a face, "It must be a hoax. They set up a projector!"

"That's what I thought but I moved around trying to block the projection and I couldn't find anything like a projector."

"What did this face say?" Rachel asked.

"There was a bit more," Clive said, "This had been going on for a few months and the young man had made recordings and measured radiation levels, temperature, pressure, that sort of thing. He was quite thorough!"

"It could still be a hoax!" Rachel persisted.

He nodded slowly, "It could be, but there is something about this that rings true. I spoke to Phil in Brookhaven about it and naturally he is full of doubt but he is going to look into the possible physics of the other universe and that may be where it will end. However, this face has said that it has met creatures on other worlds in our universe and we are trying to work out a system of directions. If that is true, it will be astounding!"

Rachel took the mug from his hand, "I think that we need more coffee!" And she marched back into the kitchen.

Clive smiled after her vanishing figure; at least she didn't say that he was crazy to continue with this!

CHAPTER THIRTY-FIVE

"We've had an e-mail from Clive," Patrick announced to Mary when they had arrived home and he had turned on his computer.

"What does he say?" Mary walked to stand looking at the screen, "That we are suitable cases!"

"No, he has a list of questions that he wants us to ask Charlie the next time he appears," Patrick showed her the message, "It looks as though he's going to follow up on this, at least for the time being!"

Mary bent and peered at the message, "I'm not sure Charlie can answer any of this! I got the impression that he doesn't know where he is; all a bit vague!"

"I think so too but we'll do as we're asked," Patrick sent an acknowledgement.

"Have you noticed that Charlie does not appear so often lately?" Mary settled down in her favourite armchair.

"I think that is because we restricted the times when we want to talk to him and where. Don't tell me you're missing him!" Patrick looked over to his companion in surprise.

"Like a head cold! I wonder if we can prevent him from appearing!" Mary said.

Patrick thought for a moment, "I never even thought about stopping him! I was curious and I still am! This could lead to a totally different type of life for us!"

"My life has changed enough, thank you!" Mary said.

CHAPTER THIRTY-SIX

Clive settled down to his normal routine of lectures and some nights in the observatory. There was little point in thinking anything about Charlie until he appeared again or Phil coming back with some ideas on the physics in the other universe.

Rachel in her supportive role would come and sit with him after the children had gone to bed. He would talk to her, not expecting an answer but just clearing the thoughts in his head.

One evening, they were doing this when Rachel interrupted his words.

"There's that buzzing noise again!"

Clive stopped and listened. There was definitely a buzz in the room, so he got up and tried to find what was causing it. It was most noticeable in the far corner and that was strange because all that was there was a bookshelf and no electrical appliances!

Frowning, he returned to his chair, "I hope that isn't a short in the wiring in the wall. It might mean having the whole house rewired!"

"It sounds more like an insect," Rachel said, "I wouldn't be surprised if there's a moth or something behind the books!"

"Or a bookworm!" Clive smiled at his own joke and tried to gather his previous thoughts.

"I think that it's louder!" Rachel stood, "I wonder if it's a nest – Oh!"

Her cry made Clive spin round in his chair and he saw what had surprised her. There was a spinning ball of lights!

Clive knew what it was but he was puzzled. How had Charlie found him? He pulled Rachel back into her chair,

"That is the alien I was talking about! Give it a few moments and the face will appear."

Sure enough, within a few seconds the familiar grey features started to appear. Clive looked at his wife and saw an expression of amazement.

Fully formed, the mouth in the face opened, "Hello Clive, how are you today?"

Rachel uttered a small eek.

"Fine Charlie but you have surprised us! This is my wife Rachel."

"Pleased to meet you Rachel. I hope that it was not too much of a surprise!" The grey face smiled.

"N – no, not at all," Rachel stammered.

"I do not understand why you should be surprised, nothing surprises me here!" the grey head said.

"Charlie, how have you found me at home?" Clive asked.

"I followed the instructions you gave me," Charlie replied.

"I haven't given you any instructions!" Clive wondered for a moment if he had and then forgotten but he was sure that had not!

There was a pause and then Charlie explained, "Sorry! That was my error! You will give me directions in your future. I find that it is difficult to match your time to mine!"

"You – you can see into the future?" Rachel managed to croak out the question.

"I can see into your future," Charlie said, "I find that an amusing activity as our time is just one, past, present and future."

"You don't have time?" Rachel's eyes were wide with surprise.

"Yes, I do have time but I see all of it at the same moment," Charlie turned his grey face towards Clive, "I will ask for directions as we will have many more discussions here. I find that Mary and Patrick are not happy with my visits but you and your friend Phil will be only too happy to see me. I hope that Rachel will not mind!"

"I don't mind but I don't want our children to see you!" Rachel said emphatically, "It will give them nightmares! Probably me too!"

"What are nightmares?" Charlie asked.

"We sleep every night and when we sleep, we dream," Clive tried his best to explain, "The dreams are just sorting out in our minds some of the problems we had while awake. Sometimes the day's events are too much and that can produce frightening dreams that we call nightmares."

"Sleep, that is something strange for me!" Charlie said thoughtfully, "I see that you are periodically inactive and wondered why. It seems such a waste!"

"We cannot go for more than a couple of days without sleep," Clive informed him, "Without sleep we become useless, cannot think correctly and have hallucinations."

"Like now!" Rachel muttered.

"How very strange," Charlie said, "I think that I now experience what you call surprise. I cannot imagine not being able to think correctly! What are hallucinations?"

"Hallucinations are when we hear and see things that may not be there," Rachel's voice had a bite in it, "like floating grey faces!"

"Is that what you call madness?" Charlie seemed oblivious as to Rachel's meaning.

"It is a form of madness," Clive said before Rachel could continue her attack, "There are many forms of dysfunction in the mind, some quite mild and others quite severe."

"Do you all become mad or only a few?" Charlie sounded interested.

"We all have the possibility of suffering from a mental disability but with most of us it takes a bad experience, such as losing someone or being attacked," Clive replied.

"Losing someone," Charlie said slowly, "Is that what you mean by death? I think that if part of me were to die, it would be a big shock, bigger than it is for you!"

"I can understand that!" Clive said, "You are all one and it would be like one of us losing a part of our brain."

"More so!" Charlie said emphatically, "I know that you operate on people who have suffered damage to the brain but most of the time you survive. With me it would be terminal!"

"Or even madness!" Rachel threw that across the room.

"Yes, a madness beyond belief but then I would quickly die and my universe with me. I have to go now and think upon these matters. Goodbye." With that, Charlie's face broke apart and vanished.

It was so quiet in the study that they could hear the sounds of the house moving slightly as though it was alive.

Rachel broke the silence first, "Well, that wasn't quite the same as E.T.! I can show E.T. to the kids but not that!"

Clive stared thoughtfully at where the face had been, "Every time he appears he gives a little clue as to his world but it's always just out of reach of a full understanding!"

"Such as?" Rachel asked for a clarification.

"If he died, so would his universe!"

CHAPTER THIRTY-SEVEN

Phil was very surprised at the news that Charlie had appeared in Clive's study.

"How did he know where to go?" His voice was muffled over the telephone.

"He says that I will give him directions in the future. I did ask him when but he just said 'not now'. I'm not sure if he meant that I shouldn't ask now or that the time was not now. All very confusing!" Clive explained, "I think that it's encouraging that he can understand directions. Perhaps we may be able to use his knowledge after all."

"I can't make out if he's time travelling or that he's aware of all time!" Phil said, "If he's time travelling that could upset the causal effect; he could break a cup and then drink out of it, assuming that he uses cups!"

"How are things among your people?" Clive was curious as to the results of Phil's students thinking of the problem.

"I'm more worried about your couple!" Phil sounded concerned, "That young man did a remarkable job for an amateur but not good enough! He recorded radiation and I would have expected that from the photons released in the room but we have no idea of what type of radiation."

Clive became serious, "Do you think that there's any danger?"

"Dunno, perhaps you should get them in to a medical unit and set up better equipment!" Phil suggested.

Clive snorted, "Where will I place the equipment? It seems that he is free to roam anywhere now!"

"Yeah, be careful! Some of the guys here have come up with some interesting theories," Phil said, "I don't want to show them the recordings; for one, we'll never keep the lid on it and I didn't want to channel their thinking in any particular direction."

"It must have been difficult to get them going without a target!" Clive said.

"Oh yeah! We had a lot of freaky ideas when we started! I just let them talk and picked up on some of the more sane ideas and it is surprising how they settled down to rationalising the idiotic from the practical!" Phil sounded amused.

"And did they come to any conclusions?" Clive asked.

"Their chief objection was that there is a lot of stuff we still know too little of and I think we can agree on that! They've gone off in separate groups, each group with a different objective. They are looking at black holes, dark matter and energy and one group raised the possibility of a Dirac Sea."

"That last is interesting!" Clive rustled some papers as he referred to some notes that he had made, "Charlie keeps emphasising that our two universes are incompatible, that neither can exist in the other. That suggests to me anti-matter and that was what the Dirac Sea was all about!"

"I don't think that it's as straightforward as that! He refers to not travelling and being one and many. We also have to think if his universe obeys the same basic conservation laws and I'm not sure if he can answer that if we asked!" Phil gave an audible sigh.

"I wonder if Charlie's universe has vacuum energy." Clive pondered almost to himself, "And there's Dark Energy and Higg's fields. He seems to be spread out over the complete space."

"I have a feeling that he will not be able to answer that! Try to imagine that you are the only thing in that universe and what you see is everything. He would have no questions, in fact the only questions he has are about us!"

"Perhaps he can't see what is there for some reason. If he didn't know there was something, he wouldn't ask questions."

"Then how did he find us?" Phil asked.

"Ah! We seem to be going round in circles!" Clive snorted, "I'll ask him anyway, perhaps he knows more than we or he realise!"

"I want to see this Charlie!" Phil said, "I won't believe it until I do!"

"You're welcome anytime, you know that, and Rachel would be pleased to see you again but I can't promise that Charlie will appear on cue!"

CHAPTER THIRTY-EIGHT

"Hells bells! I should have realised that!" Patrick exclaimed when they heard about the radiation, "I know that photons are radiation but it never occurred to me that it could be harmful!"

Clive had paid a visit to Mary and Patrick to give them the news.

"It was probably because the obvious questions were about the face," Clive gave a reasonable excuse, "I've organised that you should get some blood tests and such next week. I don't think that there is a risk."

"Why don't I feel assured by that statement?" Mary pulled a face, "I've recently had a lot of tests; they'll think that I'm a hypochondriac!"

"It's just a precaution!" Clive held out a folder, "We've come up with some more questions for Charlie. I would like to be here to ask them and maybe add a few more but if I'm not, could you do the honours?"

Patrick took the folder and started reading, "No problem! You probably won't be here anyway. Hey, this is heavy stuff!"

"Charlie has appeared in my home!"

Mary and Patrick looked at Clive with open mouths, so surprised at his statement that they failed to speak.

"It gets weirder and weirder!" he continued, "He said that I gave him directions of how to get there sometime in the future!"

Mary sat down heavily, "Oh my God! We *do* have an immortal time-traveller!"

Clive held up a cautionary finger, "Perhaps, or perhaps not! We know that he is in a different universe to ours and it is possible that the two universes contact each other at different times relative to each other. That is how he explained it."

Patrick gathered his wits, "You mean that our here and now isn't fixed in relationship to his here and now?"

Clive nodded, "Charlie said that he had witnessed things in our past and in our future. It is very possible that the contact was made in his present time but at different times in our history."

"I don't get that!" Mary shook her head, "Time's time, isn't it?"

Clive smiled sympathetically, "Imagine that you are on a train and that the window is blacked out except when the train is stationary. You are sitting still in the same place all the time but you see something different at each station. That is what is happening to Charlie, only his train sometimes goes backwards."

"I can give a better example," Patrick said, "The GPS satellites are not subjected to the same amount of gravity as we are and time is measured differently in space. They can be as much as thirty-eight thousand feet out in one day, that is about seven and a half miles and that error has to be corrected."

"No wonder people get lost sometimes!" Mary gave a short burst of laughter.

"He also said that there were other creatures, other civilisations on other planets!" Patrick said.

Clive nodded, "Obviously he can pop up anywhere in our universe. If we think of the train again, it is not just a single line but a network. The trick is to get on the right line to arrive at a predetermined destination and how he does that is what we want to know."

Patrick held up the papers, "And these questions are to find that answer?"

"And a few more!" Clive sat down, "The problem with talking to Charlie is that his references are obviously different to ours; his description of what he is and where he is for example, they don't correspond to what we believe is possible even in another universe!"

"I don't understand that!" Patrick's face screwed up, "Surely he knows what and where he is?"

"It's a matter of perception," Clive explained, "Do you really accept that you are mostly empty space and that everything around you is also empty space, held together by fields of energy? I don't think so, not at a basic level but its true none-the-less!"

"I think that he cannot answer your questions!" Mary stared at the astronomer, "He appears to live such a basic and simple existence that he has no perception of what we are talking about!"

"That is possible but he made a face and also what lies beneath a face, so he must have some sort of ability in spatial references to do that. We just have to understand that!"

"And he has to understand us!" Mary concluded.

CHAPTER THIRTY-NINE

"I just hope that this isn't some hoax!" Phil growled when he arrived from the airport in a hire car.

"From our point of view it is genuine!" Rachel smiled sweetly, "and I can't see how it can be a hoax! Good day to you Phil!"

Phil grunted and nodded, "Sorry, I forgot my manners! How are you? If it had been just one person, I would have ignored it completely!"

"Even if it were me?" Clive chuckled, "That was my thought at the beginning but I was impressed that they travelled up to Cambridge to see me and then when I saw Charlie for myself, it convinced me that even if it were a hoax I wanted to know how it was done."

"I've had those young fellows back home completely engrossed in the problem and they have come up with various ingenious theories but I will have to return them to their proper studies soon." Phil ruffled his beard and broke out in a huge grin, "What an earth-shaker if this is true!"

"Are your students all male?" Rachel asked.

"Oh no! There are a couple of young women who are very bright. They've formed an alliance against the men and they seem to be succeeding!" Phil gave a snort of amusement. "When do I meet your youngsters?"

"We can go down tomorrow if you're not too tired," Clive led his friend towards the study, "I can't guarantee that Charlie will make an appearance."

Charlie didn't make an appearance, nor had he since the last time. It was decided that Mary and Patrick would stay with Clive for a few days so that everyone was concentrated in one place. Clive's rambling old house had more than enough room.

The children had gone to bed and Clive, Phil, and Patrick were talking in the study, while Mary and Rachel were watching TV in the living room.

At first because they were in discussion, no one heard the slight buzzing and then both Clive and Patrick broke away from Phil and stared at the small sphere of lights that had appeared in the corner of the room.

Initially Phil with his back to the corner did not notice that he lacked an audience and then with no response was received he turned and stared at the dancing lights with his mouth open.

"Oh my word!" he exclaimed, "Are you recording this?"

"Only with our camcorder," Clive answered and then called out to the two women who came running.

Piece by piece the face formed, grey and blank of expression. When the face was fully formed it became animated and turned towards them.

"Everyone is here, how wonderful!" If anything, Charlie's face was even more animated than usual, it broke into a wide smile, "and you must be Phil, pleased to meet you!"

Phil failed to answer.

"Can we all sit down?" Clive dragged some chairs to face Charlie and pulled the amazed Phil into one. "Charlie, we have some questions for you, if you wouldn't mind answering them."

"If I can, it will be a pleasure!" Charlie's faced positively beamed.

"Can you tell us if you know what atoms are and how they work in your world?" Clive had dragged the list from his desk and was reading from it.

"Ah! I do know about atoms in your world," the grey face answered, "I find them fascinating but we do not possess anything like them here."

Phil gave a snort, "I find that more than just a little peculiar, it's impossible! First of all, how do you exist if there are no atoms, no matter? Secondly, if you do not have them, how do you know what they are?"

The grey face nodded soberly, "The second question is easier to answer. I have observed you over a considerable length of your time and I was watching Rutherford and Curie as they worked, so I listened and learned. Later I read your books. As to the other question, there is no matter here, at least what you would recognise as matter."

"Then tell us what you are!" Phil continued.

"I am me! I am all that there is in my world!" If Charlie had shoulders he would have shrugged them.

"If you are not matter, how can you create this face in our world?" Clive tried to stick to the notes he had made.

"I have learned how to excite the particles that you call photons. I cannot reach any of the other particles and it has taken a long time to find a way of making this shape."

Clive referred to his notes again, "We would like to find the other creatures in our universe. Can you tell us where the nearest ones are?"

Charlie's face froze for a moment as though thinking and a smaller sphere of spinning lights appeared, transforming itself into a hand with the index finger extended.

"There!" The finger pointed down through the floor.

Clive looked at his watch and scribbled the time on the notepad, "That means that it's in the Southern Hemisphere!"

"I do not understand why you would want to meet them," Charlie said, "they are not that remarkable by your standards!"

"Why not?" Clive asked.

"They are like you!" Charlie gave the startling answer.

Patrick gasped, "Do you mean that they're human?"

"No! They are solid!"

Phil chuckled, "I would be very surprised if they weren't; everything is solid in our world!"

"That cannot be true!" Charlie objected, "There are many things in your world that are not solid. That was one of the things I noticed and was originally attracted to."

"You mean energy?" Phil said thoughtfully, "Are you telling us that you are energy?"

"In a way, although it is hard for me to explain," Charlie's voice sounded puzzled, "There are many things that you have still to find out in your world, your universe and until you do my explanations will be incomprehensible!"

Phil fell silent after giving a grunt.

"What I find incomprehensible is that you're here and talking to us!" Rachel pointed at the grey face, "You are just energy and yet you can talk, you can learn and you are curious. That doesn't add up!"

"You appear to have emotions," Mary added her part, "and I have never seen electricity having an emotional fit!"

"If you recall, I said that I am not exactly as you think I should be," Charlie replied, "I am not really matter, not really energy, not in your terms. I am me!"

Phil came alive again after giving some thought to what he was learning, "When we talk to you, are we talking to your whole universe, everything that there is?"

"There is nothing else!" Charlie said.

Phil sat back in his chair and scratched his beard slowly, "What is beyond, outside of your universe?"

"What is outside of yours?" Charlie replied, "I know of nothing beyond the boundaries of either universe, nothing detectable."

Clive asked about his particular interest, "How many other different life forms have you seen in our universe?"

"I find your system of numbers bewildering!" Charlie smiled and sounded apologetic, "As far as I have gone, it must be in what you refer to as millions or billions!"

Mary's eyebrows shot up and she whispered loudly, "Wow!"

"Are there any creatures like us, human?" Patrick asked.

"I wouldn't know!" Charlie's answer surprised them all, "I don't actually see you, I sense you and I sensed the others. I copied you face as though I was using Braille, what your blind people use. I have no idea what you 'look' like and I am pleased that my attempt to make the face is accurate!"

"But you were reading my book!" Mary exclaimed.

"There are differences between the paper and the ink," Charlie explained, "These I can sense, as can any of your forensic scientists."

"Can you point to any other life-forms that you've come across that are near to us?" Clive asked.

"I can, but near to me may be a long way in your terms!"

"That is our problem but knowing where to look, where to go would be very helpful!" Clive waited and checked the time.

Obligingly, Charlie pointed to a dozen or so locations, equally distributed between the Northern and Southern Hemispheres. Clive tried to remember where he pointed but he had the camcorder to fall back on.

"I have to go now," Charlie said, "The link between us becomes tenuous. Perhaps I can come back tomorrow." With that the face broke apart and disappeared.

Clive turned towards Phil, "Well, what do you think now?"

"I don't know what to think!" Phil had slumped back in the armchair, his glasses on his head and his hands together and buried in his beard, "My head is full of many thoughts and many ideas but I still sense that there is something basically wrong!"

CHAPTER FORTY

It took Clive and Phil three days to make sense of Charlie's pointing finger and plot lines towards the distant stars. Mary and Patrick had to leave and resume working, although both thought about phoning in sick for a few days.

Clive checked the records and after a few false starts when they became very excited, they concluded that there was something wrong with Charlie's navigation.

"What I found was that there were no nearby stars in most of the places, or that there was the wrong type of star to support life," he complained.

"Life as we know it!" Phil corrected him, "It's a pity that he can't describe the life forms, at least that would give us a clue!"

"Charlie seemed so certain that there was something there," Clive sounded frustrated, "I was really hoping that we could find somewhere to concentrate our search for E. T."

"Life is full of uncertainties; no sooner do we think that we've nailed something down than we find it isn't what we thought it was!" Phil said.

"If Charlie really believed that there was life where he pointed, why would he be wrong?" Clive tapped the calculations.

"Well, we assume that he really is in a different universe and we know that there is a problem with spatial references; perhaps that's the problem," Phil suggested.

"Or it could be in the timing!" Clive's eyes opened wide, "We are being idiots! Charlie has been around for billions of years and in that time the universe has changed; stars have moved, some have exploded and new ones formed. Perhaps a billion years ago there were stars in those locations and that's what he saw then."

Phil looked over to his friend, "How are you going to prove that? Can you trace the movement of stars accurately enough to find where they are now?"

"When I asked for nearby stars, that would have meant that if they were near, they were in our galaxy and there is a chance that we can find some of them!" Clive sounded triumphant. "The only snag is working out the time period."

"You'll use computer models?" Phil asked, "Perhaps I can help in that. We can run similar programmes and see which answers coincide."

"All we need is just one sun with one planet!" Clive was literally radiating enthusiasm.

"How accurate were Charlie's directions?" Rachel asked.

"The locations will include a few suns but that is far easier to search than the billions of others in the Milky Way!" Clive sounded triumphant.

CHAPTER FORTY-ONE

Josef Kranz walked across the campus towards where his office was located with all of the others. Walk isn't quite the correct description; it was more like an amble and this was made ridiculous because of his long, thin body that gave him the appearance of a stick insect.

He was also lost in thought. Nothing remarkable in that; he had been known to attend a function without saying a word or even remembering what had been said to him or that he had been there.

The staff and students were used to this odd behaviour and accepted it with an amused smile. They also accepted his enormous intellect, which was probably why they forgave him for what in other people would have been insulting behaviour.

Despite living in his own world he had become aware that some students were engaged in an odd exercise. In itself it was not odd as students often took on side issues that took their fancy. What was odd was that they were all Phil Bissell's students and they were all involved in a similar task. Again, that was not unusual except that it was not on the curriculum and it was diverting them away from their normal studies.

He reached his door and stood still, head down for several minutes and then slowly opened the door and walked to his desk, or rather the pile of papers and books that indicated where the desk stood.

He had a great deal of respect for Phil; he had helped Josef settle in when he first arrived and the papers that he produced were first class but he was obviously up to something.

There are no secrets in any college and he had overheard what some of the students were doing. It appeared that Phil had set them on a mind game concerning possible other worlds but the baffling thing was that he had set firm parameters, as though he had something specific in mind. Josef had searched for any new discoveries or theories and found nothing that attached itself to the mind game.

Phil was ever practical, so why was he encouraging this sort of game with his students?

Josef quickly found out that Phil was in England but not at Oxford or Cambridge or any of the usual venues, in fact there was nothing happening in England for a month or so. He checked the time and worked out that it was still too early in England for a 'phone call. Later then.

He passed the time by thinking about Phil's mind game. It was certainly interesting, so much so that it was morning before he realised it. He called Phil's cell 'phone.

Phil groaned when he saw who was calling. And then putting on a cheerful voice, he answered.

"Hi Josef, what can I do for you?"

"Sorry to disturb you Phil but I heard some of your students talking over a problem that you set them. It sounds interesting and I wondered as to the reason that you set them this task." Josef asked.

Phil tried to sound normal although he was annoyed. "What problem was this?"

"It was something to do with space having few or no dimensions, at least that was what I understood."

"Oh that one! I'm trying to get them to think outside of the box. You know that I'm always complaining that they don't use enough imagination," Phil crossed his fingers.

"For no other reason?" Josef sounded surprised, "I would like to get involved and if you give me the parameters, I'd like to sort out an answer."

"Josef, I'm in the middle of something with some friends here in England. Ask one of the students for the details and I'll talk to you when I get back. Is that okay with you?"

"That's fine! I just didn't want to barge in on your territory." Josef was well aware that this could upset people.

Phil closed the 'phone and looked at Clive, "That was Josef Kranz and he wants to join in."

"I met him once or twice," Clive said thoughtfully, "I hear that he's brilliant!"

"Like a diamond! I'm still trying to keep this quiet until we know more, so the question is, should we tell him all?"

"How much does he know now?" Clive asked.

"Only the problem that I set the students but he's already wondering why I did it!" Phil grimaced.

"Well, you set the problem to bring in more minds and if he is as good as I've heard he could be an asset," Clive reasoned, "Do you want to bring him here?"

"Not at the moment, I want to see his reaction first. Can you come over to us and bring everything?"

Clive thought for a moment, "I can hand over duties for a week or two and there isn't anything pressing. I'll ring Mary and Patrick and warn them to handle Charlie by themselves and Rachel should be fine here. No problems! I can bring everything except Charlie!"

CHAPTER FORTY-TWO

Josef Kranz ambled into his office in his usual manner. He dumped his attaché case on top of the papers on his desk and then stared myopically out of the window. A slight cough brought him back to the present and he stared blankly at the two figures sitting on his sofa.

"Morning Josef!" Phil smiled at him.

"Morning!" Josef answered, "I thought that you were in… England!" He had to think of where Phil had gone.

"They have invented the aeroplane!" Phil said.

"Of course they have!" Josef acknowledged and failing to understand Phil's humour.

"I flew back last night and I brought a friend with me, Clive Anderson." Phil gestured towards Clive.

"Oh, hi! Did you have a good flight?" It was an automatic phrase and Josef wasn't interested in the answer.

Clive tried unsuccessfully to hide the smile on his face. He had come across other academics that were lost in their own world but not as extreme as this!

"We had a very pleasant journey, thank you," Phil answered, "We were wondering what you thought of our little mind game."

"Mind game?" Josef blinked rapidly, "What mind game?"

"About a different universe!" Phil sighed but patiently led Josef into why they were there.

"Impossible!" Josef stated emphatically and appeared to dismiss the conversation.

Both Clive and Phil were taken back at the conviction in Josef's voice but before they could utter a word, he continued.

"The task that you set was ridiculous! There would be no universe without matter! A universe with just permanent random energy would be invisible, of no substance!"

"Can you suspend your disbelief for a moment?" Clive said, "Try to think of how such a universe could exist."

Josef groped for his chair and slowly sat down. Clive thought that he could actually hear the gears working in Josef's skull.

Very slowly Josef set out his argument, "First of all, your problem stated that both universes were created at the same time, at the Big Bang but that is paradoxical! If that was the case, both universes would share some common factors but the rest of your problem says otherwise."

"What if both universes were created at the same time; how could the other evolve in the way we suggest?" Clive asked.

Josef stared at them for several seconds and then surprised them. "This isn't really a mind game, is it?"

Clive and Phil exchanged glances and then Phil answered, "Not entirely, no! We have found something that can only be described in the way that we have stated but we have the same problem as you in that we can't see how it could exist!"

"Tell me what you have found," Josef sat back in his chair to listen.

Clive took up the narrative, "It really found us! We have a lot of data and recordings that you should see first."

Clive then related the story to date, while Phil uncovered Josef's computer that was buried under a heap of papers and set up the programmes to display the data and film.

Josef listened intently, his expression as usual not showing surprise or disbelief. He then looked at the data, followed by the recordings of Charlie's appearances. Then he just sat still, staring out of the window and deep in thought.

Clive waited for a few minutes and then started to ask something but Phil held his hand up to indicate that Clive should continue being patient.

Suddenly Josef stood up and walked to the two enormous whiteboards on the wall. He paused for a moment and started writing mathematical formulae. Clive and Phil followed and tried to make sense of what Josef was writing. Most of it was understandable to Clive, equations that he was used to, some he had forgotten about and a few more that were entirely new to him. Eventually, most of the boards were covered with Josef's neat writing.

During this whole process no one had said a word and now Josef stood back to survey his work. Slowly he approached the board again and started striking out parts, then he wiped other sections and replaced them with new equations. Finally he stood back.

"What have you found?" Phil asked.

"I don't know!" Josef replied in a soft voice, obviously still deep in thought.

"Is it possible?" Clive asked.

"Oh yes! Kind of possible," Josef made a few more adjustments, "I am going to have to work on this a lot more. It's replacing almost everything that exists here."

"How long?" Clive asked.

"Is a Chinaman!" Josef turned to them and smiled, "In broad terms it should not take too long but working out the finer details could take years!"

"We want to keep this discrete for now," Clive said.

"In case they think we're all as mad as hatters! I understand but you had better stop those students or someone else may put two and two together." Josef pointed out.

CHAPTER FORTY-THREE

Clive hung around for a few days, meeting old friends and making new ones. It also kept him in touch with the latest projects but he said nothing about 'Project Charlie'!

Every time he checked in with Josef he was greeted with a gentle smile and the words, 'Soon, very soon,' without any further revelations.

He checked in with Rachel and was informed that all was quiet; much to her immense relief Charlie had not made another appearance. Forgetting the difference in time zones he woke up Patrick, who sleepily informed him that Charlie had not appeared there either.

Out of interest he joined Phil and the students and listened to some of the suggestions that were made. Some were sensible but way off the mark and the others were very fanciful. None of them were anywhere near the real situation. Feeling out of place, he returned home to his normal routine and duties.

A few days later he woke early and sat down sleepily to drink the first coffee of the day. Rachel joined him in the kitchen and turned on the small TV for the news. Clive's sleepiness left him in an instant!

At first he thought that there had been another terrorist attack in London as the presenter was very excited. Then the images started to appear of a huge burst of light over Nelson's Column and a distorted hum and crackle could be heard.

The presenter gabbled, "Is this a UFO? There have been lights in the sky observed over capital cities a few years ago. Are aliens trying to contact us or is this a natural phenomenon?"

Rachel's eyes opened wide and Clive thought about his efforts to play down Charlie's existence and here he was putting on a very public display! He could easily make out the individual points of light.

"That is Charlie, isn't it?" Rachel asked.

"It looks very much like him, only larger! Why has he done this?" Clive gnawed his lower lip.

Within a few hours he was receiving 'phone calls and e-mails from every source imaginable and eventually Phil called when he saw the news in America.

"Did you have any idea that this would happen?" he asked, "Everyone here is going mad, they think that it's an alien invasion!"

"Yeah, same here, and you know that the idiots will be pouring out of the woodwork! I had no idea and it's much larger than he produced before!" Clive sounded worried and with good reason.

"At least it wasn't his face; that would have created a real stir!" Phil offered the only relief that he could.

"We must be thankful for small mercies," Clive agreed with a sigh, "When he turns up here I'll have a few questions to ask him!"

Patrick rang next, "Have you seen it? We could see it from the college! Is it Charlie?"

"We think so but until we speak to him again we cannot be sure. If he appears there first, please ask him." Clive put the 'phone down and considered disconnecting it for a while.

It was almost a week later that Rachel called out and Clive ran into the living room to find Charlie's face forming. Patiently he waited until the face became animated.

"Charlie, good to see you again but you made an enormous appearance in the centre of our capital city and now everyone is asking what it was. What were you doing?"

Charlie looked thoughtful, "Can you describe what happened?"

Clive described the ball of light in Trafalgar Square.

"Ah! I think that I know!" Charlie looked slightly surprised, "I think that was the first time that I succeeded in penetrating into your world. I used an enormous amount of energy but realised that there was no need to be so generous. Since then I have used just the correct amount. Did it cause any damage?"

"It caused a lot of idiots to claim that we were being invaded and a few heart attacks from the shock!" Clive said angrily.

"I heard that a few cars collided because the drivers were looking the wrong way!" Rachel added.

"I am sorry, it was a miscalculation on my part," Charlie managed to look contrite.

Clive thought for a moment before uttering a sound, "Charlie, if that was the first time you came here, what have we been doing up to now? These other times were earlier than this huge display?"

Charlie smiled, "That is correct! Our two universes touch at random places and at random times, only until now have I been able to exercise any control over the sequence. I have said that before, haven't I?"

"You can't tell me how you control this sequence or even what the method you use," Clive reconfirmed earlier statements.

"I move towards you to bring us together and then I just project the image!" Charlie sounded apologetic.

"You don't use a machine?" Clive frowned. This sounded more like mysticism!

"I don't know how to make a machine! I have seen how you make machines and I would like to do so but our worlds are so different that the same principles do not apply."

Rachel leaned forward and pointed at Charlie, "You have said that you can now control how you appear here; does that mean that you can select anywhere and at any time to appear?"

"Yes! I told you before that for obvious reasons I cannot tell you about the future. I also have some problems in understanding what I see in the past, so that I cannot explain what has happened." Charlie explained.

"Why can you not understand what you see?" Rachel asked.

"You are totally unlike anything that is familiar to me. The reasons that you do things would make no sense in my world!"

"What sort of things?" Rachel continued.

"You kill each other! If I did this here it would be like killing me!" Charlie sounded almost as if he were in pain.

Rachel nodded, "There are people here that think something similar. You also said that you do not die, so does that mean that you have always been in existence?"

"Ah! From my point of view that is so but time is so different here and it's hard to explain." Charlie sounded apologetic again.

"We think that time is relative," Clive explained, "Every person experiences the passage of time differently, depending on where they are and what they are doing."

"That may be because you are distinct individuals, but we are me!" came the unhelpful reply.

Clive rubbed his forehead, "In a way that makes sense. If we consider all creation, you and us, that would make you just another individual that would experience time as we do, relatively."

"That does appear to contain some logic!" Charlie beamed a smile.

CHAPTER FORTY-FOUR

Phil rang a few days later. "Clive, Josef has come up with a scenario. Has Charlie made another appearance?"

"Yeah, and he added a few things that start to make some sense – kinda. What does Josef say?"

"It's a bit complicated," Phil said, "Would Rachel mind a couple of guests until we can speak to Charlie again?"

"I'll check but as far as I know it will be okay." Clive wondered what ideas Phil and Josef had come up with. "It sounds intriguing!"

"It is, and you can tell us what Charlie said," Phil fixed a date and replaced the telephone. If Josef was right, it would shake up the scientific community and some of the religious ones too!

When they arrived and Josef stepped out of the hire-car he gaped at the rambling Victorian structure. "I thought that when you said that the appearance was in the study that it was at the campus or is this part of the university?"

"No, it's Clive and Rachel's home and here they are," Phil took Josef's arm and pulled him forward to introduce him to Rachel who was waiting with Clive.

They settled in the kitchen, Rachel making a pot of coffee, a large pot as she knew that this would be a long session.

Clive repeated what Charlie had said during his last appearance, Josef nodding slightly as he listened.

"Now, what's this great theory you've thought up?" Clive asked.

Josef shifted in his seat as though it was uncomfortable, "That's it, just a theory! From the initial conversations it would appear that none of the physics of the other universe were anything like ours, so we could not understand at all but I've tried to explain it in our terms how we could understand it."

"But he emphasised the difference," Clive objected, "He even said that he cannot relate to anything here!"

"He probably can't!" Josef blinked thoughtfully, "but that doesn't mean that there are more similarities between the universes than we were led to believe. If we start at the Big Bang, where he says that his universe was formed at the same time as ours, there is a natural progression, an evolution where suns and planets are formed but we also think that many of the other universes formed at the same time failed to progress further. It is also possible that some failed to evolve in the same way as ours."

"I think that Charlie said something on the same lines, that his universe evolved differently," Clive reminded them.

Josef nodded, "He did say that but if we think about it, the energy and matter must have evolved somehow, in some way that Charlie can talk to us. That evolution must resemble ours in some way and so I tried to apply our knowledge to his state of existence."

"And what did you find?" Rachel topped up the coffee mugs. What she heard next almost made her spill the coffee.

"He is an infant!" Josef didn't show any sign that this statement was remarkable.

Clive raised his eyebrows, "If he's an infant, where are the parents?"

"The Big Bang is his parent! When the event happened, his universe didn't clump together to make matter, it remained as a form of plasma and probably not quite the plasma that we would understand." Josef didn't appear to realise the nature of the bomb-shell he had dropped.

Clive groped for some explanation and then grasped on something, "We think that Dark Matter is what made our universe clump together to make suns and planets. What if his universe didn't have Dark Matter?"

Josef nodded again, "If we did not have Dark Matter, how would the original plasma evolve?"

"It is conceivable that there would have been some collecting together of atoms and particles that would have created a life form," Phil had already thought this through, "but without a strong local attraction of gravity they would not have formed dense matter, such as planets and suns."

Rachel still stood with the coffee flask in her hand, "How can you have life without matter?"

Josef lightly coughed, "It is a difficult concept but it is possible and I'll give you some examples. If local gravity fields vanished here, the galaxies, suns, and planets would start to break up and the matter that they are composed of would spread out to fill the void between the galaxies. Space isn't empty, it is full of energies and a thin smear of particles and that thin smear would thicken up considerably if all of the matter was spread uniformly."

Phil broke in, "These particles would be attracted to each other and repelled as they do now, but those energies in particles are very short ranged; only gravity has a long range effect."

"But how can you say that is life?" Rachel objected.

Josef pointed to his own head, "Think of the brain. How is it that it passes messages from there to every part of our bodies? It's just a lump of fat but it enables us to be who we are as individuals."

"Are you claiming that it uses electricity to pass messages from one part to another?" Rachel looked astonished.

"Maybe not electricity, but energy most certainly," Josef replied, "The smallest particles, the quarks communicate with each other and the other energies and particles that make up everything. There is every reason to suppose that the same happens in Charlie's universe, it's almost inescapable!"

"So Charlie's universe consists of just a soup of particles spread out over the entire volume of space?" Clive said reflectively.

"But why does all this make him an infant?" Rachel asked, "From what has been said, he's fourteen billion years old!"

Patiently, Josef led them through the explanation, "From an evolutionary point of view he has never developed from the earlier stage. He is probably as basic as life can be! Consider that life here developed from a cocktail of chemicals, through single-celled creatures, multi-celled creatures to the primitive life forms, and eventually through to us, Homo sapiens. Charlie never had that and that's why he finds us so fascinating!"

"How does he know where we are and what we look like? He doesn't have any eyes!" Rachel complained.

"All of those energies I've been describing. Our universe emits huge amounts of radiating energy and this is what he probably detected in the first place," Josef gave another small smile, "As for having no eyes, we don't know that but those small short-range energies could easily be used to describe a face and what lies beneath. Particles vibrate from the sounds that we make and he could detect that and recreate a voice."

"You make it sound so plausible but I'm not convinced!" Rachel finally set the coffee flask down and resumed her seat.

Clive had been lost in thought and now stirred, "Our universe is expanding. I would think that Charlie's universe is also expanding."

Phil answered, "Almost without doubt, which means that Charlie is expanding and getting thinner!"

Clive shook his head, "I was thinking further than that! We, our sun, is a second or third generation star, born out of the evolutionary process and the destruction of one or more other stars. Our universe cycles its matter and energy, recreating life as it does so. Charlie is composed of the original matter from the Big Bang!"

Josef sat back in his chair and took a sip of coffee before answering, "What happened to that early universe with its giant stars?"

Clive frowned, "They blew up! I just said that novae created our sun!"

"And how long did those ancient stars live for?" Josef continued his questioning.

"Some, the largest only lasted a few million years, the others probably no longer than a few billion years," Clive was still trying to see what Josef was getting at.

Josef nodded, "They collapsed due to excessive mass created by gravitational fields. Charlie doesn't have gravity!" He looked amused as he stared over the rim of the coffee mug at his companions and their startled expressions.

Clive was the first to break the silence, "I was thinking that as Charlie doesn't have suns, then the energy and matter would not be recycled, but now you suggest that it is a constant level of energy over the past fourteen billion years!"

"Not quite!" Josef placed his mug down carefully, "If Charlie does not have Dark Matter, and he may not have Dark Energy either! We know very little of what they could be!"

"But Dark Energy is what is making our universe expand, that we know! If he doesn't have Dark Energy then it is possible that his universe is not expanding beyond the initial expansion of the Big Bang!" Clive looked surprised at his own words.

"It may even be collapsing!" Josef pointed out, "It could have already collapsed!"

CHAPTER FORTY-FIVE

That suggestion created a long silence, while they thought through the implications and exchanged glances, as though trying to read the other's minds.

It was Rachel who started them talking again, "If it has collapsed, how can we still be speaking to him? Is he a ghost?"

Josef shook his head slightly, "He's not a ghost and in his universe all is well, but that may have been billions of years ago in the time-line of our universe!"

Rachel shook her head furiously, "That's nonsense! How can he be alive and well there, but dead and buried here?"

"You're probably thinking of another universe as another galaxy, far, far away." Josef quoted from a well-known film and smiled as he did so. "It's much further than any other galaxy, but at the same time just here," Josef stretched out his hand, "just beyond our reach. It does not share with anything in our universe and that includes time."

Phil was stuttering with excitement, "W-we are forgetting something! Gravity effects time and if there is a high gravity influence, like on a black hole's event horizon, time is drawn out and anyone there will experience time extended. Charlie has a low gravity influence, almost zero and that should result in a shorter time compared to ours!"

Josef was nodding, "I haven't forgotten about that aspect, however, the gravitational effect is so minimal that time may not exist at all or have other strange qualities."

Clive turned towards his confused wife, "Charlie's universe has its own laws and its own time. Do you remember that he keeps saying that he cannot explain to us his notion of time and Josef is suggesting that at Charlie's particular time may correspond to anywhere on our timeline."

"Clive understands it well, "Josef said, "Our two universes are moving constantly relative to each other. Charlie has somehow managed to control that process, which is quite remarkable!"

"But he's dead!" exclaimed Rachel.

"Not to him! I think that the concept of death didn't occur to him until he met us or other creatures like us."

Phil tried to help Rachel out, "Think of a film; we know that Humphrey Bogart died long ago but we can still see and hear him, pushing boats up rivers and walking off into the mist. The only difference here is that Charlie is still alive in his world."

"Think of Charlie as an old movie, that's weird!" Rachel gave a slight shudder.

"So how do you describe Charlie?" Clive asked Josef.

"He is a primordial, physically undeveloped being. Very intelligent, his contacting us shows that, and despite his assumptions of being immortal, he has a life time shorter than fourteen billion years, maybe even less than our solar system!"

"Poor Charlie!" Rachel pulled a face, "What if you're wrong?"

"We'll find that out when we speak to him." Josef asked for a refill of his coffee, apparently unconcerned with his statements.

CHAPTER FORTY-SIX

Several days later Charlie made an appearance.

"I have had a lot of trouble making contact with you," he complained, "Perhaps we are drifting too far apart."

They had all gathered in Clive's study, forewarned of the appearance by the usual buzzing that brought the girls running in from the garden. Josef kept staring as the face formed from the swirling lights as he groped blindly for a chair.

"How are you today Charlie?" Clive asked.

"I just said, I'm having trouble making and keeping contact!" For the first time Charlie sounded angry and hurt. Clive then remembered that Josef called Charlie a child. Was this a childish tantrum?

"Well, you made it and we have some more friends for you to talk to." Clive pointed out Josef and Phil.

"Hello Phil, nice to see you again and greetings Josef." Charlie's mood changed and he produced a smile.

"We've been discussing you Charlie," Phil announced.

"Is that why Josef is here?" Charlie's grey face turned towards Josef.

"Hello Charlie!" Josef smiled and was startled to receive an answering nod from the disembodied head. "You are full of mysteries and I was called in to try and answer some of the questions."

"And what are your conclusions?" Charlie sounded almost coy.

"They are not conclusions, just theories. I think that you are made of similar stuff to ourselves but your universe lacks some of the things we have and that's why you're different to us." Josef stated and leaned back in his chair.

"Is that the only difference?" Charlie's face resumed a calm expression.

"That's the main one and it explains everything else," Josef felt uncomfortable at the thought that this being was long dead.

"Such as I/we cannot live in your world," Charlie agreed. "We cannot understand why you have achieved so much and yet you cannot see into your future and have an imprecise knowledge of your past, or why you are confined to your small world."

"We have a few ideas about your world," Phil said softly, as he knew that he had to reveal something very shocking and he did not know how Charlie would receive it. "One of our ideas is that your universe has never developed very far from the point of creation and that's why you have no stars and planets."

Charlie's face froze, indicating that he was holding a conversation with himself. Clive wondered what it would be like to talk to his own big toe, then he mentally shrugged the image away.

When Charlie's face re-animated, it had a mournful expression, "Are you telling us that we are not very old?"

Phil nodded, "If that idea is correct, then you are probably only a few million years old. We could be wrong," he hastened to add, "but the lack of suns and planets indicates that you lack what we call Dark Matter and Dark Energy. As we understand it, you need those to form stars and planets."

"And you think that means we have not evolved as you have?" Charlie still looked mournful. "Perhaps we are as old as we think without evolving as far as you have."

Josef spoke up, "You could be right! We don't know enough about that subject to be positive but we think that they should appear automatically and very early in the creation event. It could be that you are as old as us but lack those dark forces."

"I'll have to get back to you. This is a lot to consider." Charlie's face began to break up and melt away.

"That went well!" Clive said sarcastically when the last vestige of the face had disappeared, "I expected a much longer conversation."

Josef shook his head, "He has something really big to think about, possibly the hardest thinking he has ever done. As we cannot examine his world, he has to compare our ideas to his reality."

CHAPTER FORTY-SEVEN

Mary had become accustomed to spending her evenings with Patrick, although he spent three evenings a week with a night-school class. Those evenings were very lonely, so empty of any company that she even started to wish that Charlie would make an appearance, but he did not. She had no idea of what had been discussed with Clive and the others, so she was unaware that Charlie had some deep problems.

She could have joined her girlfriends but they somehow appeared to have changed, then she realised that it was she that had changed. She had a new perspective on life, that somewhere there were other creatures that she could not imagine or really comprehend, living on worlds that defy thinking about.

Her conversations with Patrick were about Charlie's world and she took books out of the library concerning alien life forms and even a few science-fiction stories. At work she became quieter, so much so that Mr Priestly asked almost every day if she felt well. In truth, she was feeling suffocated; hemmed in with a knowledge that she could not easily share with others.

She surprised Patrick with the announcement that she was going to spend a few days in Paris. She had to get away and gain some stability and in the French capital she could ignore the foreign conversations around her. She stayed for a week!

Patrick understood how she felt, at least in part. He realised that she had been an independent person with her feet planted firmly in this world, but now she had been exposed to a surrealistic world where everything that she had believed was in contradiction. He felt somewhat shaken himself.

On her return he kept out of her way; they shared the evening meal and watched the TV, which she didn't really pay attention to, or talked when she wanted. Eventually, she burst out with her feelings as Patrick hoped she would.

"Is Charlie real? I cannot accept his world; it has no substance! I cannot see how anything can exist without being solid," she waved aside the explanation that he was starting to express, "Yes, I can accept that our world is not really solid and that there are huge spaces between atoms, but at least our atoms are held together to give some semblance of solidity, of reality!"

Patrick paused to see if she would continue and then asked, "Are you horrified at the thought of living in his world?"

"I'm not living in his world! I believe that there is something basically wrong about his description! He appears to be an intelligent mist and I cannot accept that a mist can be intelligent!"

"If you can come up with an alternative answer, I'll listen but at the moment we just have to accept his description." Patrick paused, "I'll ring Clive tomorrow and see if he has any news."

Clive surprised them both with an invitation for the following Saturday. It would appear that he had a lot to tell them. Patrick informed him of Mary's feelings and Clive became silent for a moment.

"Rachel has also expressed some doubts, so I'm not overly surprised," He hummed briefly, "I'm not sure if what we have to say will settle her mind but we'll try to help."

It was Rachel who opened the door and whatever it was she was thinking, she hid it well and gave them both a big welcoming smile.

"They're in the study," she informed them, "I'll make some more coffee. Would you like to help me?" she asked Mary.

Mary was surprised at the number of people gathered in Clive's study; both Phil and Josef rose to greet her. She was introduced after placing the cups and coffee on the table and given a chair.

Patrick brought her up to date, "They have been talking to Charlie quite a few times and the results are surprising!"

"You're going to tell me he's a hoax!" Mary ventured.

"No, no, he's real enough!" Josef informed her, "I worked out some possibilities as to what he and his world could be and I presented them to him. He went away to think about them and he has come back to ask a few more questions. We are hoping that he will make an appearance this weekend and continue the ideas."

Patrick shifted on his chair, "What sort of ideas?"

Phil took up the narrative, "When Charlie started talking to us he claimed that his universe was created at the same time as ours and in the same event. Since then, the two universes have evolved in different ways and that is what we have been speculating about."

"So you haven't got firm ideas, just guesses!" Mary looked and sounded sceptical.

"We can't examine his universe as we can our own," Clive explained, "Our only contact that we can examine is Charlie and even that is an indirect contact. The questions we have put to him will hopefully provide answers that agree with our 'guesses', as you put it."

Josef nodded vigorously, "He further said that the only thing contained in his universe was him or them; there are no suns and planets, things that he thinks are wondrous and that means that there cannot be centres of gravitational energy, Dark Matter. We have only discovered Dark Matter and Dark Energy fairly recently, so we do not fully understand them but it appears that Charlie's universe contains nothing that ours contains beyond the primordial matter."

"Dark Matter and Dark Energy were created in our universe at the same time as everything else and our stars and galaxies appeared very quickly after the event, the matter attracted to where Dark Matter had concentrated." Clive added,

THE Dancing Lights

"Charlie's universe appears to be stuck at a stage that ours was only a few million years after creation."

Josef continued nodding as Clive explained and added, "Without Dark Matter, his universe cannot evolve, but there is more! After the creation event our universe expanded, as would happen after any explosion, but after that, Dark Energy kept that expansion going so that our universe is the size it is now and it is still expanding. Charlie's universe cannot be very large in comparison with ours, maybe about thirty light years across."

"I have been doing a lot of reading lately," Mary crossed her legs, "and as I understand it, these ideas of Dark Matter and Energy are just that, ideas. We have observed some anomalies and placed these names on certain characteristics but we still know almost nothing about them."

"We have to go with what we know and understand at this time," Phil acknowledged with a smile, "otherwise we could end up like our ancestors and creating myths. The other thing is that by studying a universe without Dark Matter may help us to understand ours better."

"But you just said that you cannot make a study of Charlie's universe!" Mary exclaimed with a slight frown.

"We are doing it by proxy!" Josef explained, "Charlie is doing the study for us, with a little help and prompting."

"This question about Dark Matter has another interesting aspect," Phil said, "Ever since Einstein presented his view of the universe, we have come to the conclusion that time is strongly connected to gravity; various experiments in changing gravities have led to changes in the time recorded. Charlie's ability to 'see' time differently to us may be because he has no Dark Matter and probably no gravity."

For the first time Patrick entered the conversation, "You said at the beginning that Charlie claimed that our two universes were created in the same event. Can you explain that?"

"There could have been more than one creation event!" Clive stated, "That would explain why his universe is so different. Whatever caused the event in the first place released tremendous energies and that cause may have led to multiple events. It's just an idea!"

Patrick nodded slowly as he absorbed the idea, "So what conclusions have you arrived at concerning Charlie and his universe?"

Josef settled back in his armchair as he prepared to explain the enigma called Charlie. "To begin with, neither Charlie nor we are sure of how old he is! That problem is because his idea of time and events is so different to ours and if his universe started at a different event, we have no starting point. It could be that he is the same age as us, fourteen billion years or just the age of our solar system, four and a half billion years, or even just a few million years old. If he had suns and galaxies we could make a stab at an approximation based on the life cycle of stars but that is impossible! If we accept Charlie as an isolated case, then the question of age is irrelevant, it probably is anyway. Without clumps of Dark Matter, the ordinary matter is spread more or less uniformly through space and over the period of time that his universe has existed, the matter has linked together and created a consciousness, a sentient being."

"What Josef has not mentioned is that Charlie in many ways is a child!" Phil looked amused at the thought, "If you think of our own children, they appear undeveloped and we watch them mature into adults. Charlie has not had that development; without external stimulus, he has remained as an infant or juvenile!"

"An infant that can create nightmare images, I can't believe that!" Mary questioned.

"I can believe it!" Rachel expressed a snort of laughter, "They will experiment with everything that they find; our children certainly do! If Charlie is a thinking being, he will also be curious."

"But how does he do that?" Patrick asked, "If we cannot reach into his world, how does he reach into ours?"

"We have no real idea," Josef admitted, "All that I can think of is that what he has available, energies that can affect our matter and energies but not vice-versa. How he can do that without any machines is a real puzzle!"

"So let me get this straight," Patrick held his hands in front of his face, "We have one universe appearing with suns and galaxies, and another that is what, a mist?"

"Probably more like a thin soup!" Josef said.

"And the one made of soup is far smaller than the one with suns, is that right?" Mary still had a small crease between her eyes.

"And it is younger than ours!" Patrick added.

"Forget the age," Phil instructed, "We assume it is younger because it has not developed to the same stage as ourselves but we know why that is, no gravity which means no entropy, no time!"

"It does lead us, me at least, into a strange conclusion," Josef said quietly, "If it has been around at the creation event and not developed, it could be just a few million years old and collapsed because of the lack of development. It may have vanished fourteen billion years ago!"

Mary shuddered, "How can we talk to something that died before the time our solar system didn't exist?"

"Ah! That is difficult to visualise," Clive leaned back and stared at the ceiling, "Charlie does not occupy the same space and time that we do, that is a certain fact, and the two universes slide past each other and probably even through each other. Because the matter in both universes does not react to each other, we would not be aware of each other. Somehow Charlie can catch a glimpse of us and he has amplified that to produce the images. This means that although he may have died a long time ago, that is only a maybe, his universe still exists and not connected to our time and space."

"I don't get that!" Patrick hunched forward, "He said that he can see all of time, I guess he means his time, so why does he not know that he is dead?"

There was a long silence, broken by Rachel pouring more coffee.

"He hasn't mentioned it!" Phil looked surprised, "Perhaps he does not understand it."

"I have another answer," Josef mused, "Charlie's world has no time. According to our theories, no gravity, no time, so his world just is, without beginning or end."

Mary gave another shudder, "I think that is worse! Imagine that you don't know that you're dead! That is called purgatory!"

"Isn't that a definition of a ghost?" Rachel smiled at some inner thought.

"Now people," Clive remonstrated, "I said that we should not involve myths and fairy stories!"

"It might explain some of the ghost stories," Rachel persisted.

"You mean that some of Charlie's efforts were mistaken for ghosts?" Phil laughed, "It is possible and a piece of unexplored science, in which case it is not a myth!"

"I certainly thought that when he first appeared to me!" Mary muttered and shuddered as she recalled the events leading up to today.

"Anyway, our ideas appear to have possibly upset Charlie, if he can be upset, and he has gone off to find out." Clive wrapped up the discussion and they broke up to walk in the garden, except Josef and Phil who continued their own arguments.

CHAPTER FORTY-EIGHT

"I wonder about Charlie's psychology," Phil leaned forward, "If he is a reasoning being, then he may have the same hang-ups that we have. Perhaps he has gone away to sulk!"

Josef had his eyes closed, his head resting on one hand and appeared not to have heard Phil. Just as Phil was about to repeat the thought, Josef spoke.

"The reason that we have 'hang-ups' is due to our experiences, going as far back as primitive life. The ancient life forms lived in a savage and competitive world, the ultimate consumer society. Survival and evolution depend on those characteristics and we have never really questioned those, so they remain in our make-up. Without those we would not ask questions and aggressively explore or invent things."

Josef opened his eyes and looked directly at Phil, "Charlie's world, his universe is not competitive! All the parts are connected and that prevents competition; if each part knows what the others are thinking and doing, there is no need to compete as no one can win! He/they are intelligent, excessively so and curious. He asks intelligent questions about the strange radiations emanating from our universe and others, things from outside and he does not question the things inside; there is no need to do that because he is aware of everything there is to know. Now he has come across us who forces him to consider his own self; we are in effect the adversity that he has lacked until now!"

Phil had listened intently and now began to realise what they had done. "We are creating the type of world that we evolved from; an aggressive, vicious world that will produce the hang-ups that we suffer from."

Josef smiled, "We did this the moment that we talked to him! Up until then he had lived a peaceful, sedate existence but we have changed that! If you remember your biblical education, you will remember that Adam and Eve were cast out of Eden because they gained knowledge. Charlie's world we can think of as Eden and we have forced him to question his own existence, to gain dangerous knowledge!"

Phil blinked! He had not considered a biblical connection but Josef had introduced an intriguing thought! "Is Adam about to be cast out of Eden for the second time? I can see where you are going with this; Charlie is not dangerous at this moment, but now he sees that time is finite and his own death may have already occurred due to things outside of his universe and therefore, out of his control. That will develop into a sense of insecurity and a whole series of hang-ups. Poor bugger!"

Josef had continued smiling as he listened to Phil expound his thoughts and now he extended a finger towards his companion, "How does it feel to be the Serpent in the Garden?"

Phil rocked back into his chair, his eyes expressing his horror. "What have we done? Can we salvage anything? Perhaps if we explain to Charlie that there may be problems and we are here to help – if possible!"

Josef slowly shook his head, "Once the seed is planted, its roots spread very quickly and firmly. From what I have seen of therapy, there may be more harm than good and we have the additional problem of dealing with something totally alien."

"You're saying that we should just wait and see; is that wise?"

"Charlie may as yet surprise us!" Josef took another coffee and grimaced as he took a sip, "It is cold! He has developed a gentle curiosity with none of the aggression that we display and it may well be that he will find his own solutions."

Phil snorted, "Perhaps he can teach us how not to be so aggressive!" Then he gave a louder snort, "My therapist lives in another world! I think someone has already suggested that therapists do live in cloud-cuckoo land!"

"You are anticipating the worst! I'm sorry that I mentioned it!" Josef patted Phil's arm, "You had something to say about Charlie's psychology; what was it?"

"Damned if I can remember!" Phil pulled at his beard, "Ah, yes! I was considering the idea that he is an infant and until now he has had everything his own way. When our infants are confronted with opposition, they throw a tantrum. Can Charlie do that and just what sort of tantrum?"

"Hmm, that is close to what we were saying just now," Josef said, "He has not shown any sign of temper so far but the same applies to our children, until something happens. Usually that is because the parent misunderstands or neglects something in the child's routine. I don't think that will happen as his species lacks that aggressive gene."

"I bloody hope so!" Phil sighed, "I cannot see what we can do to calm him down."

"Of course, in this situation we can be considered to be acting as his parents," Josef said so quietly that Phil could just hear him, "and as I have just pointed out, the child usually throws a tantrum because of a foolish parent!"

CHAPTER FORTY-NINE

Charlie did not appear that day. Mary and Patrick booked in at the local inn as there were too many people in the house for sleeping. They left it until the last moment, hoping that Charlie would make an appearance and in the morning they looked the worse for wear.

"I can't sleep in a strange bed!" Mary complained.

Patrick surveyed her face as they took their places for breakfast; it was obvious that she had hardly slept.

"I usually can sleep anywhere but I think that we are also trying to place Charlie in some mental compartment," Patrick said and ordered coffee for them both.

"The trouble is that these professors are so convincing and they make him out to be like us," Mary grumbled, "and I can't accept that!"

"Ah! You must accept that he is something but it's difficult to think of him as anything else but as a human face. I think that is the main problem; because he appeared as a human, we cannot accept that he is some vague, formless creature from way out there!" Patrick eyed the menu, "Are you up to a full breakfast?" Mary shook her head and ordered some toast and Patrick did the same, plus some more coffee.

When they arrived at Clive's house, Rachel was just leaving with the children as she thought that it was best to get them out of the house and avoid Charlie. She was going to take them into Cambridge to do some shopping.

The professors were waiting for them in Clive's study. It was obvious that Phil and Josef had sat up for most of the night, possibly all night, arguing various theories about Charlie and the universe. They had been writing formulae on the whiteboard, wiping out the scribble and replacing them with new scribble and there were books and papers strewn everywhere. Patrick cleared two chairs by dumping books and papers on the floor.

"I suspect that Charlie had not thought of anything on the lines that we suggested," Phil was saying, "He was drifting along quite happily just being; it must have been a shock!"

"I was drifting along quite happily too," Mary said with some chagrin, "and I wonder if Charlie is any better off for knowing; I don't think that I am!"

"I think that must apply to most of the human race and aliens too!" Clive agreed. "No one wants to think too deeply about what is really there."

"You're saying that ignorance is bliss!" Patrick said and Clive nodded.

"I don't like surprises and would prefer to know what was coming..." Phil broke off as they heard the familiar buzz.

Charlie appeared from the usual swirl of lights. His grey face looked slightly different; some emotion, if he had any, was evident.

"Hello!" Charlie looked at them one by one. "I/we have been examining your ideas and have come to the conclusion that basically you are correct."

Phil looked surprised, "I didn't think that you would reached a conclusion so quickly!"

Charlies face broke into a smile, a sad sort of smile, "When your world is as small as ours, it does not take long to explore."

"So your universe is smaller than ours?" Mary burst out.

"Oh yes, a lot smaller!" Charlie then turned towards Josef, "I am amazed that creatures such as yourselves can have such ideas! You have described us accurately without being able to see or touch us and that is beyond our capability."

"Just how accurate are we?" Phil asked.

Charlie's face froze for a moment and then gave a slight nod, "It is difficult to translate our world into terms that you would understand; however, I will try. Our universe is somewhere between the size of your solar system and your galaxy, maybe a bit larger and we cannot detect any shrinking!"

Everyone was surprised at his last statement; Phil and Clive leaned forward, while Josef leaned back and stared at the ceiling and contemplated the ramifications. Mary and Patrick just stared open mouthed at the grey head.

"Your universe is not shrinking?" Mary said quietly, trying to imagine living on a never changing world.

Charlie's head nodded, "We cannot detect any change in our size but that may be due to other factors. However, we have a vague proof that our universe collapsed millions of years in your past!"

Mary looked shocked and grasped Patrick's arm. "How can you have disappeared and still speak to us?"

"Our time is without the same parameters as yours," Charlie smiled, still a sad smile, "for that reason we cannot be sure if that the figure I have just given you is correct."

"I can believe that!" Josef spoke to the ceiling, leaning further back on his chair, "It would take an appreciable time for you to evolve into a consciousness and three or four billion years seems about right."

"I still don't get it!" Mary frowned ever deeper, "You died out before our sun appeared, before there was life on this planet! How can you be talking to us?"

"I think I can explain by giving an example from our universe," Phil turned to Mary and Patrick, "We see galaxies on the edge of our universe and that light has taken billions of years to reach us. In that period the galaxies have changed, they have moved position and most will no longer exist; they have evolved along with everything else, going through their life cycle but we can still see them today. Charlie's universe in some respects is even further away and we can still interact with his in the same way we can still see the far galaxies."

Mary started to understand and the frown disappeared. Patrick crossed his legs and stared at the grey image.

"There is not a lot more for us to talk about," Charlie announced, "so this will possibly be the last time we will meet, although you may detect our earlier transmissions in your future."

Clive and Phil almost jumped out of their chairs. "You can't just go away!" Clive waved a finger at Charlie, "I am sure that there is still a lot more we can learn from each other!"

"But we cannot learn anything more from you!" Charlie's great head looked sad but resolved, "Our worlds are so different that we cannot apply lessons across the gulf that separates us."

Phil and Clive started yelling at the grey head but it had already started to break up and the dancing lights were disappearing. Charlie had one last thing to say.

"Goodbye and thank you!"

Everyone was struck dumb, Clive and Phil stood with their arms raised and the mouths open and unmoving like some park statues.

"Well, I'll be damned!" Patrick said softly.

"I'm not surprised!" Josef had brought his gaze down from the ceiling and had a strange smile on his face, "We had revealed the truth about his world, a bitter truth that if it had been us we would have probably reacted in the same way. We removed the mystery and the beauty, that sense of contentment that all is well and will remain so. We had introduced the concept of change."

Mary stared at Josef, "I feel an immense feeling of grief, as though it was the passing of a dear friend. That is extraordinary! From the time he first appeared he has created a lot of horror in my life but I will miss him!"

Phil placed things in perspective, "I feel the same but at the same time I feel enriched by the experience; would we have ever come to the conclusions that we did without that experience? Could we have considered such an ephemeral creature as Charlie?"

Josef nodded, "I suspect that he has similar feelings. Clive has his SETI targets, if they prove to be correct and Charlie has revealed that the true meaning of life is far more subtle and complex than we ever would have believed. We have also revealed to ourselves the sad demise of an extraordinary creature, so we mourn him."

"May he rest in peace!" Patrick muttered.

Rachel shook herself from a shocked trance, "It was all so sudden! There is one hope, one legacy he has left to us; that there is other intelligent life out there. We do not know the form of that life; perhaps it is as bizarre as Charlie or even more so but he told us that it exists."

Mary stood up, "I'm all for finding it and if possible, to make contact with Charlie again."

"Perhaps not!" Phil looked around the group, "Josef and I were talking earlier about Charlie's psychology and we came to the conclusion that the contact will have profound aftershocks in his universe. Any contact between species will be the same; look at what happens in our world when two civilisations meet for the first time."

"Are you saying that we should not seek out new worlds?" Mary sounded indignant.

"'And boldly go where no one has gone before'," Phil smiled at the quotation, "No, it is in our nature to explore but perhaps we will be more careful in seeking and revealing the truth to those we meet, perhaps even to ourselves. Truth can be a powerful and dangerous weapon!"

CHAPTER FIFTY

Charlie didn't leave immediately; he had one last visitation.

James Nettles was very sick. He had been found lying by the side of the road and at the point of death. The emergency crew kept him alive and delivered him to Telford Hospital where he was revived and appeared to become his old self.

After a thorough examination, the doctor's gravely shook their heads. The abused liver was completely useless and his other organs were failing. It was just a matter of time before the spark of life would depart.

James was placed in a small ward where three others were beyond any assistance. On the third night the nurse heard him softly singing and when she checked he was awake and conducting an orchestra that only he could see and hear. She smiled and returned to her desk. If she had stayed for a few minutes longer she would have witnessed the 'orchestra', a burst of light in one corner and the dancing lights whirling in a silent symphony.

James Nettles passed away listening to the music of light.

THE END

THE DANCING LIGHTS

ABOUT THE AUTHOR

Mike Williamson was born in London in 1943. At the time, his father William was a sergeant in the Royal Engineers 'somewhere' in Scotland, and his mother Violet was an artist.

After the war they settled in London and Michael surprised his parents by learning to read at the age of three. By the age of seven he was reading everything he could lay his hands on, and in the local market he found a treasure trove... pulp fiction! Most importantly he read Astounding Science Fiction and Fact and many other similar magazines. To a boy living in a city recovering from the nightmare of bombardment it was a wonder. Here there were other worlds and other times, futures that stretched the imagination, and the articles by Dr. Willy Ley explained why they were possible.

The nearest thing to space flight in the 1950s was aviation, and so he joined the Air Training Corps, eventually becoming top cadet before joining the RAF. He enjoyed flying, but while he was doing this, the USA and USSR were achieving the impossible, launching men into space and eventually standing on the Moon.

On leaving the RAF, he joined some of the companies in the aerospace industry, making electronics, engines, and even the whole machine. During all of this time he never lost his interest in science fiction or the science behind it. He wanted to write, but work and life was a necessary obstruction. It was not until he retired in 2003 that he could settle down and concentrate on his first love.

His passion is shared with his wife Lucy (They met while both were living in Sweden) and she has a scientific education, which helps when he often goes astray. Now he lives a few miles from the Cambridge Observatory, UK and gets first hand information.

..

Made in the USA
Charleston, SC
26 March 2013